GIRL

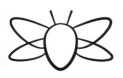

Benjamin Harper
Sarah Hines Stephens

Illustrated by
Anoosha Syed

[Imprint]
MAKE YOUR MARK
NEW YORK

A part of Macmillan Publishing Group, LLC

Library of Congress Cataloging-in-Publication Data

Names: Hines-Stephens, Sarah, author. | Harper, Benjamin, author.
Title: Bug Girl / Sarah Hines Stephens and Benjamin Harper; illustrated by Anoosha Syed.
Description: First edition. | New York : Imprint, 2017. | Summary: "A girl who loves bugs discovers she has some of their super-hero like abilities when an evil scientist tries to take over her hometown"—Provided by publisher.
Identifiers: LCCN 2016014025 (print) | LCCN 2016026349 (ebook) | ISBN 9781250106612 (hardcover) | ISBN 9781250106605 (Ebook)
Subjects: | CYAC: Insects—Fiction. | Ability—Fiction. | Monsters—Fiction. | Magic—Fiction.
Classification: LCC PZ7.H574 Bu 2017 (print) | LCC PZ7.H574 (ebook) | DDC [Fic]—dc23
LC record available at https://lccn.loc.gov/2016014025

Our books may be purchased in bulk for promotional, educational, or business use. Please contact your local bookseller or the Macmillan Corporate and Premium Sales Department at (800) 221-7945 ext. 5442 or by e-mail at MacmillanSpecialMarkets@macmillan.com.

Book design by Ellen Duda

Imprint logo designed by Amanda Spielman

Illustrations by Anoosha Syed

First Edition—2017

1 3 5 7 9 10 8 6 4 2

mackids.com

If this book you think to steal, think again, 'cause here's the deal:

Sticky fingers will be reimbursed with foul haircuts and footwear cursed.

Fashion disasters will also give grief to any who choose the life of a thief!

To all the dorks, geeks, pre-hippies, science
nerds, protopunks, gothlings, and other
glorious misfits that populate the pariah table.

B.H. & S.H.S.

ponytail

homework
(completed)

Members
Only jacket

bug button
collection

awkward
stance

Trina
(Madagascar
hissing
cockroach)

Dragonfly
action hero
lunchbox

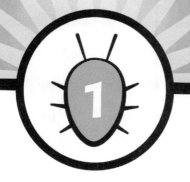

Amanda Price's day was going as expected. Terribly. It was presentation day in biology, and Amanda had prepared what was, in her mind, a masterpiece explaining one of the many wonders of the natural world. She knew from past experience, however, that her fellow sixth graders at Oyster Cove Middle School would probably feel differently.

When Mrs. Mallard called her to the front of the room, Amanda took a deep breath and gathered her visual aids. All around her she could hear the rest of the class fidgeting nervously in their seats. Some students eyed the door, ready to sprint for freedom if things got out of hand. They knew something icky was about to happen. Something that involved an unsettling number of legs.

It was well known that Amanda was a bug expert. Insects, arachnids, and other arthropods were her hobby—her whole life, really. Her bedroom was lined with tanks housing rare

species of bugs, and most of the books on her crammed shelves were dedicated to her invertebrate obsession.

It wasn't a typical pastime. Amanda didn't know many girls (or boys, for that matter) who truly *liked* spiders and ants. But Amanda didn't just like them. She loved them. She loved them so much that whenever she could, she focused her schoolwork on her favored subject. *Praying Mantises and You*, *The Plight of the Tarantula*, and *Tree Lobsters: Where Are They Now?* were just a few of the reports she'd given in Mrs. Mallard's biology class in an attempt to help others appreciate the wonder of bugs. With eager

THE TENACIOUS TREE LOBSTER

By Amanda Price • Sixth Grade

The amazing tree lobster, otherwise known as the Lord Howe Island stick insect, was thought to be extinct for nearly eighty years. Last seen in the 1920s, a small population of these incredible creatures was discovered recently beneath a spindly bush on the top of a craggy volcanic island. The tenacious tree lobster lives!

Tree lobsters are large—about the size of a human hand—resemble sticks, and have many other unusual features. For example, though female tree lobsters can reproduce without males (this is called parthenogenesis and allows small populations to survive), male-female pairs form strong bonds, and the males follow the females from activity to activity—the couples do everything together!

anticipation, she'd stood in front of the class and allowed walking sticks or luna moths to cling to her arm, only to watch her classmates emit horrified moans and make barf faces at one another.

"I've got the vapors!" Amanda recalled Sheila Swaddles swooning from the back of the class during one of her more memorable presentations.

Yet Amanda felt certain that one day, something would spark the interest of one of her classmates, and her work would all be worth it.

She had hoped that day would be today, and she had prepared a report titled *Madagascar Hissing Cockroaches: Misunderstood and Magnificent*. It was perhaps her best report to date, and she could hardly wait to deliver the astonishing information she'd gathered. But before she had even finished the introduction, Amanda heard sniffling from the back row. *Allergy season*, she thought hopefully as she moved on to her next index card.

The class seemed a little less agitated as Amanda detailed the classification of her favorite cockroach in relation to the wider world of insects. In fact, some students even looked as if they might be learning something from Amanda's lecture. But then she stepped closer to the small tank she'd brought and kept covered with fabric. With a motion that made it look as if she were a magician revealing her latest trick, she swept off the cover. There in the tank were two of the biggest Madagascar hissing cockroaches ever to crawl on the East Coast. They were the size of doughnuts. Black, shiny doughnuts.

Amanda smiled to herself. The silence in the room indicated that her classmates were also anticipating what was to come. She removed the lid of the tank.

"You're not actually going to touch those," Wayne Guttles blurted out. "Are you?"

Of course she was. Her grade depended on a top-level presentation, and she hadn't yet held her pets that morning. Without hesitating, Amanda reached into the cage and grasped one of the gigantic bugs before plucking up its friend with her other hand.

She continued with her report, explaining how the creatures' exoskeletons were so strong that it was hard to crush them. The words were barely out of her mouth when a girl in the front row began openly sobbing.

Amanda ignored the interruption. She needed to focus. The best part of her report was coming up. "The Madagascar hissing cockroach makes its signature sound by forcing gas through breathing pores, or spiracles, located on its thorax and abdomen," she stated, and held up her favorite specimen, Trina, for the class to see.

"You mean it farts?" Darren Dibbles asked. He snickered loudly. Mrs. Mallard stifled the class clown with a look that would curdle milk and then turned it on the rest of the room. It worked.

The students were almost completely silent when Trina hissed.

Until that moment Amanda thought the wide dislike of roaches was simply a PR problem—the bugs had a bad reputation. They needed better marketing to overcome their association with filth. But the horror they elicited was made very clear when Killer, the second cockroach, let out a loud hiss of his own. The arthropods' disturbance signal created such an intense reaction in the room that the school nurse had to be called to dispense mass first aid.

Amanda returned her pets to their travel cage while all around her, students tried to recover. They wiped tears from their eyes, slumped limply on their desks, or sniffed smelling salts. Once the cage was covered, Mrs. Mallard quietly requested that Amanda not bring live examples in the future. "Never again," she said softly.

But it was already too late. Glancing around the classroom, Amanda knew her fate was sealed. She had been unpopular *before* starting this amazing report—but now things were going to get worse. Way worse. Amanda wished she had a magnificent uncrushable exoskeleton like Trina's. Based on the glares she was getting from her classmates—the ones who were still conscious, anyway—she felt like she might need it.

MADAGASCAR HISSING COCKROACH

Fun Bug Fact: Madagascar hissing cockroaches create their celebrated "hiss" by forcing air through small breathing holes called spiracles.

2

To avoid confrontation and to calm her nerves, Amanda made her way to the back of the class. Aside from being Amanda's favored place for public humiliation, Mrs. Mallard's room also hosted the sixth graders' ongoing biology project. The science teacher had brought each of her students a tadpole, and they were raising them in individual fishbowls. Once the tadpoles had matured and transformed into baby frogs, the class was going to release them into the pond behind the school.

Thanking her lucky stars for the chance to take care of an amphibian (and for a break from the commotion), Amanda huddled over the round containers lining the back of the classroom. While most students thought of their tadpole duties as a chore, Amanda loved her future frog, whom she'd named Cletus, and took her duties as Cletus's foster parent very seriously.

Dropping a piece of wilted lettuce into the water for Cletus to nibble, Amanda tried not to think about the roach situation. The tiny plump tadpole bobbed back and forth, nipping at the leaf. Amanda could not help but worry about his future. What if a fish ate him before he could swim away?

"I want you to be one of the strong ones," Amanda said into the bowl. "You will need to fight. Nature is hard."

Behind her, a throat cleared. "Are you talking to a tadpole?"

Amanda recognized the mocking voice before she turned. It belonged to Emily Battfield, Amanda's former best friend and the main cause of her descent into the popularity dumpster at OCMS.

"Oh, I was just feeding him, and he looked lonely,"

perky blond hair

naturally symmetrical features

entitled facial expression

DIGGORY by DASH floral romper (spring collection)

fresh mani-pedi

strappy sandals

rolly backpack

Amanda responded quickly, hoping that would wrap up the interaction. She tried to avoid talking to Emily.

"Here." Emily held out a pink envelope decorated with glitter and fat red plastic hearts—a party invitation.

"You shouldn't have," Amanda mumbled, meaning it.

"My mother insisted," Emily shot back with equally biting honesty. "It's tomorrow. Nice report, by the way."

With that, Emily turned around and sashayed back to the group of popular girls sitting in desks on the other side of the room. She was their reigning queen.

Amanda looked down at the invitation. The corners were worn. It had been in Emily's bag for a while. When she looked up at the girls, she found the whole pack staring at her with expressions so intense they could rot fruit.

"Oh, hooray," Amanda mumbled to Cletus. Emily's

IT'S
Emily's Birthday!
You're Invited!

dreaded birthday party. Amanda had known this was coming. She was invited to Emily's celebration every year and used to look forward to it. But that was before.

Staring at the brightly decorated invitation, Amanda couldn't help wondering, like she often did, what it was that made Emily turn on her so quickly and so horribly.

As far back as Amanda could remember, Emily and Amanda had been friends. Best friends. But on the very first day of middle school, everything changed. *Everything.* It was as if each student had gotten a memo over summer break notifying them that their elementary school life was over and they all had to start acting and dressing differently.

Well, except for Amanda. Somehow she had missed that memo and had shown up at school with a Dragonfly action hero lunch box and an adorable matching outfit. Amanda had thought her ladybug-print ensemble was cute until she stepped into her first class and Sissy Saffron blurted, "Late for preschool?" At that very moment, her classmates erupted into cruel laughter, and Amanda understood that things were different.

With a sigh of relief, she had spotted Emily sitting on

the other side of the room—someone she could count on! She was so happy to see her pal, she'd pretended not to notice that Emily was laughing, too, and hurried over. But Emily had put her hand on the empty chair.

"It's saved," she'd said.

"For who?" Amanda had asked, taken aback.

"It's just saved," Emily had responded a little more quietly, looking down. And that had been that.

Her best friend had dumped her.

Though Amanda had never been able to figure out what exactly had triggered Emily's sudden change of behavior, as time passed, she'd learned to accept it. If only she had been able to avoid it, too.

Looking into Cletus's bulging eyes, Amanda tried not to sigh. She was more than a little sick of reliving that moment, but it was hard not to when she was forced to see Emily so frequently. . . .

"Heavens to Betsy, somebody's getting big! And, Matilda, are you losing your tail?" A cheerful voice interrupted Amanda's sad thoughts. She whirled to see the saving grace of her sixth-grade experience cooing at his own tadpole: Vincent Verbiglia, who had arrived to class tardy, carrying a late pass (allergy shots) and a Megawoman action hero lunch box. Amanda beamed.

"Oh! I am soooo glad you're here," she whispered.

The well-dressed boy was a sixth-grade science geek with a fragile constitution, near-crippling allergies, and a soft spot for cats, eighties music, and fashion. Amanda and Vincent often huddled together in the hallways, did homework in the afternoons, or just sat on the Prices' porch swing and contemplated the universe. Vincent, along with Amanda, was a founding member of the Oyster Cove Entomological Society (a generic collection of geeks with an impressive title). And he had even been picked to represent OCMS at this year's Future Scientists Kiosk at the upcoming Oyster Cove

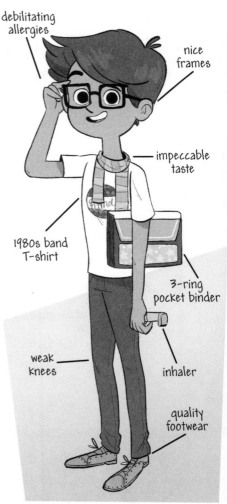

debilitating allergies

nice frames

impeccable taste

1980s band T-shirt

3-ring pocket binder

weak knees

inhaler

quality footwear

Day celebration, where he was planning to present his thesis on negative electrical charges in nature—a thesis that could earn him a hefty scholarship. He was an ultrabrain and had a permanent seat at the pariah lunch table. And he was pretty much Amanda's new best friend.

"Why, look at Cletus! He's practically a frog!" Vincent clapped like a happy parent while Cletus made small ripples on the surface of his bowl. Then Vincent noticed the mood in the room. He bit his lip. His eyes were full of concern. "Was your report received with the usual level of . . . approval?"

"Don't ask." Amanda shook her head and then tilted the gaudy invitation in her hand so he could catch a glimpse. "Plus, this."

Vincent nodded knowingly.

At least Amanda had someone who understood how much she dreaded extracurricular time with Emily and her klatch. That alone made Amanda feel a teensy bit lighter, as she gave her tadpole a last loving glance and returned to her seat.

3

When the bell rang for lunch, Amanda hoped the excitement surrounding the highly anticipated and fast-approaching Oyster Cove Day would keep news of her cockroach situation confined to room 12B. She prayed to the universe that the main topics of conversation in the halls would be students' entries in the Krafters Korner competition or how fat the animals they were entering in the Porky Pet Parade were. Rides, fun houses, deep-fried foods. Those things.

But no. Amanda was the one and only topic on everyone's lips. Gossip in middle school spread faster than desert locusts—that means *FAST*.

The instant biology was over, her classmates had run screaming out of the room, and news of what had happened traveled through the hallways. Amanda was barely out Mrs. Mallard's door when she heard the whispers of

"Bug Girl" accompanied by snickers and fingers pointing directly at her. It took three minutes for Trixie Symcox to get up the nerve to call Amanda "Bug Girl" to her face.

And once Trixie Symcox did something, everyone did it. That was just the way school worked.

"Ignore them," Vincent commanded, pushing Amanda past a gaggle of laughing seventh graders. (Even the seventh graders were involved—this was *bad*.) "Let's get to lunch. I'm starving!" he insisted.

Amanda and Vincent found their way to the outcast lunch table, where a handful of their socially awkward sixth-grade friends had already gathered. *At least things can't get any worse*, Amanda told herself as she opened her Dragonfly lunch box. If only that were true. She was removing her food items one at a time when it happened.

The plastic container her mother had filled with homemade banana pudding malfunctioned. The lid popped right off, spilling slimy yellow-and-brown goo across the table. And as that pudding oozed onto the seat and ultimately to the floor, there was a chain reaction, exactly the type of thing Amanda tried her hardest to avoid.

First, Yelba Marcos, one of the school's nosiest popular kids and also a world-class tattletale, spied the situation from across the cafeteria. Unable to resist what she saw as an amazing opportunity, she sprang into action.

"Oh. My. God. Amanda barfed! BUG GIRL BARFED!" Yelba screamed, popping up and pointing to the other side of the room. Amanda, meanwhile, was frantically trying to get the uncooperative pudding back into its container.

But it was already too late.

"Bug Girl barfed!" students started shouting in unison. "Bug Girl barfed!" The chant increased in volume, repetition, and pitch until it reverberated like speakers about to blow out at a concert. "Bug Girl barfed!"

Then the lunch monitor, Mrs. Ladles, added to the horror by storming up and down the cafeteria aisles waving her hands and shouting. As usual, everyone ignored her commands.

The commotion grew until it resembled the now infamous chaos of the "Lunch Meat Riots" that had happened when the cafeteria staff accidentally scheduled

Tuesday in the cafeteria!

The Wonderful World of Bologna!

Meat Mysteries Revealed:
How do you pronounce bologna?
Why is it spelled like that?
What exactly are "ends, bits, and trimmings"?

Featuring Chef Hoagie Joe's World-Famous Bologna Boats!

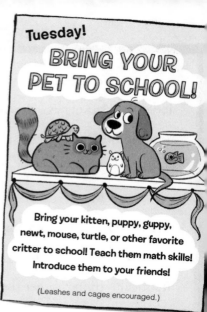

Tuesday!

BRING YOUR PET TO SCHOOL!

Bring your kitten, puppy, guppy, newt, mouse, turtle, or other favorite critter to school! Teach them math skills! Introduce them to your friends!

(Leashes and cages encouraged.)

"The Wonderful World of Bologna" on the same day as the annual "Bring Your Pet to School" event. The aroma of the featured Bologna Boats entrée (fried lunch meat topped with a scoop of mashed potato, plus cheese) created a canine frenzy that had lasted a full four hours. Amanda hoped this mob madness would end more quickly.

"*Bug Girl! Bug Girl!*" Students banged their trays on the table for effect.

It still could be worse, Amanda thought. . . . She'd managed to avoid having a school nickname for nearly two semesters. And "Bug Girl" was a far cry better than some of the insulting labels she'd overheard (like Gaggy, and Dumpers, and Crud Bucket, and Zits McGillicuddy, and Underarm). Besides, in many ways, the name was accurate. She *did* love bugs.

"Just ignore them," Vincent said, loud enough for Amanda to hear him over the din. He did not make eye contact. They both knew that the best way to deal with this sort of bullying hysteria was to pretend it wasn't happening. Any show of horror or protest would prolong the episode. And there was no point in any of Amanda's fellow outcasts standing up for her—they would only add fuel to the fire. So the entire Oyster Cove Entomological Society simply sat and waited for it to end.

Amanda inhaled and exhaled slowly. She was strong enough to handle this, she knew.

But was she strong enough to handle Emily's party? She wasn't so sure about that. More than anything, she wished she could curl into a tight little armored ball, like a pill bug, and stay that way until Sunday.

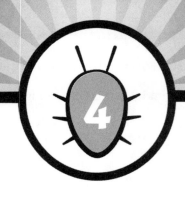

Swaying gently on her front porch swing, Amanda closed her eyes and tried to focus on the noises around her. The choppy spray of sprinklers and the hum of cicadas promised that summer vacation—a time when Amanda would be temporarily free of nastiness—was just around the corner. Summer daydreaming was the last in a long line of distraction tactics Amanda had spent the day practicing in order to keep her mind off Emily's birthday bash.

She'd tried everything. She'd even spent forty-five minutes flipping through TV channels searching for the cartoon that used to make her deliriously happy when she was in grade school. *The Most Righteous Action Adventures of Dragonfly and Megawoman: Oyster Cove Defenders!* had been her absolute favorite for years. The fast-paced show was based on the real-life historical adventures of the town's

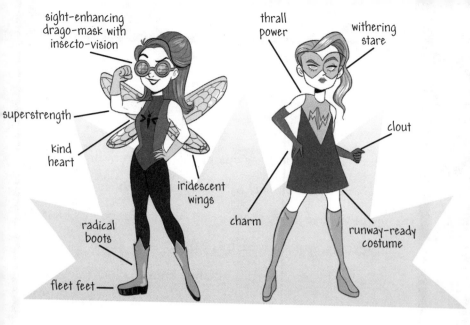

sight-enhancing drago-mask with insecto-vision

superstrength

kind heart

radical boots

fleet feet

iridescent wings

thrall power

withering stare

clout

charm

runway-ready costume

very own superheroines! And each week Amanda would wait by the TV with a healthy snack to see what kind of dastardly lowlife her favorite guardians would foil. Sadly, the animation had become quite hard to find. Even library copies of the show were worn to shreds.

But today of all days, Amanda felt like a small glimpse of those wondrous women battling evil—right here in her own hometown—might give her strength. Instead, searching online in vain made her feel worse. In spite of the fact that Dragonfly and Megawoman fought for respect, decency, and kindness, and always, always won . . . they'd been pretty much forgotten. Forsaken by their followers.

Of course, the pair hadn't actually been seen in real life for over a decade. Their absence led some folks to believe that the heroes had up and abandoned their town. Others claimed the city's champions were in hiding. And there were even kids in Amanda's class who thought, in spite of vintage video footage and firsthand accounts, that the amazing women were made up!

In her heart of hearts, Amanda knew the heroes were real. She hoped someday to see, live and in person, Dragonfly's powers of strength and flight and the withering stare Megawoman employed to stop criminals cold. But first, she was going to have to deal with this birthday party.

"Ready?" Amanda's mother asked, stepping outside and jangling her keys.

"Mom, do I really have to?" Amanda asked. Slowly she got up from the porch swing. "You know she hates me."

"Yes, you have to, Peanut," her mother responded. "It won't be so bad."

Amanda shuffled toward the car. She figured the party could go one of two ways: She could either be the main focus of the other girls' attention and they would spend the entire evening insulting every aspect of her personality, or the other guests would actively ignore her, making her sit alone and stare off into space. Either way, the trendy girls would intentionally make the fun they were having seem even *more* fabulous in order to make her feel even *more* horrible.

As they pulled out of their driveway, Amanda saw glowing yellow dots blinking on and off at the edge of the thick woods beside her house. The fireflies' dance transfixed her. She loved fireflies (after all, they were insects) and looked forward to their return each summer. To her, they were magical and wondrous, a prime example of how amazing nature could be. When she was younger, the other kids in the neighborhood used to run around and catch them, shoving them into jars, and then . . .

It was hard for Amanda to think about. She'd told the other girls that glowing nail polish wasn't worth what they were doing to those beautiful bugs. She could hear herself saying it in her head, even now. *For your information, that stuff is called luciferase, and fireflies produce that to attract members of their own species,* she'd announced as the other girls applied the bioluminescent goo to their fingers. Not one of them shared her concern.

"Mom, why do you make me go to Emily's when you know she and I don't get along anymore?" she asked, turning away from the window.

"You know, when kids are your age, they're, well, going through changes," her mother tried to explain. "And that's what's happening with Emily. She's dealing with adolescence in her own way. She doesn't *really* hate you."

Amanda didn't buy it. Wasn't thinking you hated a person the same thing as actually hating them? And why didn't adults understand that not everything that happened in middle school could be explained away by *hormones*?

"I know she hasn't been very nice lately, but Emily will get over it, you'll see. You've been friends since you were babies. She won't just throw that away." Her mother gunned the engine and shot through a yellow light. "It's important."

"But why is it important?" Amanda asked, unconvinced. She suspected it was because her mom was big on maintaining connections, and no connection was bigger than the one between her mom and Emily's. The ladies had been best friends forever, since before Amanda's father died (which happened so long ago, Amanda couldn't remember him at all). The two moms' bond was why Emily and Amanda were practically forced into being friends. And they *had been* friends. But now they *weren't*.

"Don't fret, Buttercup. Just cut Emily some slack. When the time's right, you'll know," Amanda's mother replied, implying bigger things. Amanda wished Emily would cut *her* a little slack. She nearly said something but stopped herself as the security guard standing watch outside Emily's gated community waved them in.

I must be like the wasp beetle, Amanda told herself. If, like the brave wasp beetle she admired, she could accurately resemble the more dangerous party guests, there was a chance they wouldn't recognize her as an easy target. It was a slim chance, but it was the only chance Amanda had.

WASP

Fun Bug Fact: The wasp can sting multiple times, and it bites!

WASP BEETLE

Fun Bug Fact: The wasp beetle doesn't bite or sting, but its wasplike coloring makes you think it might!

5

mily lived in one of those newer and extraordinarily pricey neighborhoods chock-full of large McMansions. Langoustine Estates, this one was called.

Even by megahouse standards, Emily's home was colossal. It was quite possibly the biggest house in Oyster Cove, built with the money her father had stockpiled after accidentally inventing some sort of computer-chip thing.

Amanda felt her stomach churn as they turned off Scallop Drive and made their way up a seahorse-shaped court, passing tacky mollusk statuary and crustacean-shaped planters. When she finally stepped out of her mom's economy hybrid onto the Battfields' driveway, she could hear the shrill shrieks of sugared-up girls mixed with the sound of laughter and backed by an obnoxious pop soundtrack. From the outside, at least, the party sounded dreadful.

Amanda's mom jumped out of the car, pulling her gym

bag over the backseat, and rang the bell while Amanda shuffled closer, looking desperately for an escape.

"Karen!" Emily's mother belted, opening the door and grabbing Amanda's mother in a powerful hug. "You look fabulous! Come in! Come in! Amanda, the kids are in the family room." Mrs. Battfield dismissed Amanda with a wave of her wrist before taking Amanda's mother by the arm and dragging her off into the dark inner reaches of the labyrinthine house. She was talking very fast about the kids being "fine on their own" and "something brewing." Probably coffee. Though Amanda thought Mrs. B was acting like she'd had quite enough caffeine.

Amanda stood in the large foyer listening to the mothers' voices fade. She paced and then kicked at the wall, wishing it would stop time. Because she knew that as soon as she stepped into the other room, it would be just like school. Horrid.

She was considering hiding behind the huge potted plant in the hall and waiting it out when the mothers suddenly reappeared.

"Sugar Beet! Why are you still standing here?"

"Where are you going?"

Mrs. Battfield held up a silver-studded gym bag. "We're going out. I'm just dying for your mom to try this new yoga-pi-latte method class I've been doing at the Om Shanty," Mrs. Battfield gushed. "It's ah-maaaaazing."

Amanda's mom nodded in agreement. "Now go on and play with the girls, Peach Blossom!" She gave Amanda a tender shove. Frida, the Battfields' housekeeper, silently appeared to help escort Amanda toward the festivities.

With a sad glance back, Amanda allowed herself to be gently pushed around the corner. The brightly lit room looked like a war zone. The remnants of a piñata explosion covered the floor and furniture; candy and toys that had been picked through and rejected speckled the shag carpeting. Pillows and shreds of wrapping paper dotted the den in a haphazard fashion. Frida looked at Amanda. The dark-haired woman didn't utter a word, but Amanda felt somehow bolstered, like she might be able to endure this moment after all.

Wasp beetle, Amanda thought, remembering her camouflage tactic. *Maybe I can go unnoticed. Maybe I can just sink into the carpet with the cast-off piñata innards and wait for my mom to retrieve me.*

Maybe. If she was lucky.

But Amanda was not lucky.

"Ooooohhh. Look who's here," Prissy Jo Feingold cooed, making Amanda's presence known. Every head in the place turned. Amanda looked over her shoulder for Frida, but she'd disappeared noiselessly, leaving Amanda to face the party alone. She stood by the counter, where the party mix and punch bowl sat.

"Happy birthday, Emily," Amanda said softly, spotting the guest of honor on the far side of the room.

The group reacted as if Amanda had run into the center of the celebration, performed a triple twist, and blown her nose, single-nostril trucker-style, onto the carpet. They all stopped what they were doing and stared at her, horrified. She heard the words "Bug Girl" being whispered—always followed by an "eww." Time stood still as she waited to see what would happen next.

"Oh. Hi," Emily said unemotionally. She turned back to what she'd been doing without making eye contact.

One by one the other girls followed her example, turning their backs, as well.

Amanda let out her breath in a grateful sigh. Though she had not passed herself off as one of them, it appeared they were going to ignore her.

Alone in the crowd, Amanda turned her attention to the buffet. There were lots of goodies to choose from, including seven different types of cake. There was a healthy-looking vegan carrot cake made especially for Sadie Bimmins, who had never tasted anything having to do with the animal kingdom (Amanda often admired Sadie's lifestyle choice but wished that Sadie

included humans in her list of animals to be cherished); a beautiful, tiered vanilla cake with artisanal sugar flowers; and even a dark-chocolate cake with chocolate frosting and curled chocolate shavings on top.

The chocolate had clearly been the party favorite. There was only one piece left. Amanda reached for it, happy to have something to enjoy at this party, even if it was only cocoa and butterfat. But before she could slide it onto her plate, it was snatched away from her by one of the other guests.

"Oh, sorry, did you want that?" Calypso Jade asked as she took a bite. She squished up her face in fake pleasure. "It's soooo good, I just had to have another piece." Calypso was notoriously mean, so her cake snatching wasn't a surprise to Amanda at all. Just another disappointment.

"Whatever," Amanda responded under her breath. She'd have the vegan cake. It didn't look too bad. And there was plenty of it. But as she prepared to get a piece of the cruelty-free concoction, Lorricent Grandy pushed it away from her.

"You don't really need to eat any cake, you know,"

Lorricent said, making an obvious show of checking out Amanda's body as if it were something to be pitied.

"Okay, I get it," Amanda said, holding up her hands. "You don't want me here. I don't want to be here. So why don't you just go do what you were doing and I'll stay out of your way?" she suggested. It wasn't that difficult. She took a few steps toward a chair in the corner. She did not hear the irritated intake of breath.

"Who do you think you are, telling us what to do?" Calypso hissed, showing lots of chocolate on her teeth.

"Seriously, Dumpelstiltskin . . . don't *ever* talk to us like that!" Lorricent shrieked loud enough to draw the attention of all the girls in the room.

Amanda sensed Emily on the far side of the party turning in her seat. She swore that she could feel the heat of Emily's stare, two grape-size circles of hot anger boring into the skin of her scalp, before she even looked up.

As Amanda tried to slip around Mikki Folders—another hostile party guest—without touching her, Mikki extended her Mary Jane–clad foot, sending Amanda hurtling toward the buffet table. Amanda collided with the

counter, elbowing the huge bowl full of sherbet-and-soda punch. It fell, spewing orange foam all over the snack mix, the curtains, and the expensive carpet. Amanda toppled with it.

Mikki, stunned by the success of her prank, let out a whimper and sank to her knees beside the other girls, who had all begun to emit a bizarre noise that was a hybrid of laughter and fear.

Emily stood and planted her feet firmly shoulder-width apart. "Why do you have to ruin *everything*?" she demanded, as if the fall were Amanda's fault and lying in a puddle of orange foam was something she was enjoying and had maybe planned.

Stomping her foot and placing her half-eaten slice of cake on the coffee table, Emily took two steps closer. Amanda squirmed in the sticky puddle, struggling to right herself. The fact that Emily was freeing her hands added to Amanda's unease: Something bad was about to happen. Amanda crawled to the far corner of the room and pulled herself into a molded plastic chair.

Unmoved by Amanda's act of surrender, Emily

continued to advance. "Every time I try to do something nice, *this* happens!" she screamed.

Emily was getting to the point of no return in her tantrum, Amanda could tell. Her face had gone from its usual milky glow to a hue similar to cranberry sauce, and her eyes looked as if they could light fires. Amanda had seen Emily mad many times before. But never this mad, and she could not predict exactly what was going to happen next. She looked around, searching for cover.

One thing Amanda knew for sure—when Emily was angry, the world needed to steer clear. The girl enjoyed throwing things. She was skinny as a rail but had a hidden strength and extraordinarily accurate aim when angered.

Emily crossed the room to the table where the cakes were displayed. She plunged her fingers into the frosting and pastry, but just as she was about to hurl two huge balls of floury, sticky fury, she paused. Something was wrong— everyone in the room could feel it. For several seconds it seemed as though time stood still.

Then the entire house started to shake. Stacked plates, cups, and silverware clattered. The legs of the rosewood credenza threatened to buckle, and hanging light fixtures swung like pendulums. Blaring car alarms and horn blasts rippled through the neighborhood a moment later. All the girls scrambled for cover as the room trembled, scattering pictures and dishes to the floor.

The shaking subsided after the longest minute of Amanda's life, but an eerie green glow remained, pulsating almost like a heartbeat.

And then the screaming started.

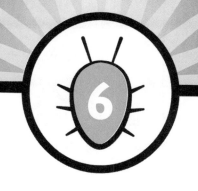
manda could not see. Clawing at her eyes, she scraped away some fallen dessert. When her vision cleared, Amanda surveyed the damage. It was bad. The room looked like a battle had been waged within its walls—shattered vases, toppled chairs, and tangled beaded curtains littered the parlor. The dust in the air glowed a hazy avocado as the light from the outside worked its way in.

Struggling to push the couch away, Amanda stood up. She swabbed the remaining cake from her face with her sleeve. Around her, other girls were flailing. Their high-pitched shrieks made Amanda wince.

Quickly, Amanda made a check. She swept the room with her eyes, taking a mental inventory—all the guests were safe with their limbs in the right places. She may have wished many of them permanently silenced, doomed to bad haircuts, or cursed with ill-fitting footwear—but

she didn't wish any living creature bodily injury. It simply wasn't in her.

The green glow continued to pulsate as Amanda became aware that the terrified screams were coming from outside as well as in. Whatever was happening, it went beyond this room, and it did not sound good. It sounded, to put it plainly, terrifying.

But for some strange reason, Amanda's curiosity overwhelmed her fear. Something within her was compelling her to run outside into the fray to find out what was going on. She didn't just *want* to, she *needed* to.

Without hesitation, Amanda darted past stunned girls and fallen furnishings. The closest exit was an open window over the credenza. Amanda leaped onto the sideboard, popped out the screen like she'd done it a thousand times before, and hurled herself outside.

Thud! She landed in the middle of Mrs. Battfield's postage-stamp-size Zen garden—winner of Oyster Cove's prestigious Garden Guru Peace Cultivator award—nearly squashing a bonsai sequoia and scattering the carefully raked patterns in the gravel. She didn't have time to contemplate her offense to serenity, however. She had to find out what was making everyone hysterical.

The screams grew in number, a rising chorus of terror, as she hustled toward Prawn Parkway. The green light that had seeped inside Emily's house glowed even more brightly outside. It drowned all other colors in its wretched hue and made Amanda feel slightly ill. Then, as she reached the street, Amanda detected a new sound in the din: the thundering footfalls of a stampede.

Before she could gain her bearings, a flood of people poured over the hill toward her, panicked and practically trampling one another in their haste to flee.

And then, with a terrific roar, the first glowing monster made itself known to Amanda. Its gaping fangs lunged ahead of a snakelike body, skeletal wings, and at least ten long, hideous legs. It snarled over the herd of hapless citizens of Oyster Cove as it continued on its path.

"Oh, snap." Amanda blew out all her breath.

Amanda paused by the rail of the overlook at the end of Prawn Parkway. The hillside terrace afforded residents a view of Oyster Cove's urban center. From there, she could see the entire town sprawling out to the bay. And peppering every neighborhood like a bad rash were glowing green globules.

Just below her in Saltwater Flats, giant scaled yetis zoomed after scrambling children. Twisted dragons soared on bony wings, maws agape, toward petrified people in the Munch-n-Bowl parking lot. Creatures that looked like a cross between tyrannosaurs and vampire bats hovered in alleys and around corners, cutting off escape routes.

It appeared that the entire city had been invaded by glowing monsters! But what were they? Where were they coming from? And what did they want?

Nearby, somebody shrieked, and it sounded oddly familiar. Amanda turned in time to see one of her Entomological Society fellows, Sh'Shelle Domalie, dive under a parked truck, narrowly avoiding the tentacles of a giant furred cephalopod. Amanda hustled over.

"Are you okay?" She squatted down, yelling to be heard in the chaotic din.

Sh'Shelle was a mess. Her hair sprang out in all directions and her cheek was scratched. "I was just doing some

advance reading and my cat started howling to get out,"
Sh'Shelle cried, brown eyes brimming. "But when I went
to let Fudgie into the yard, that whatever-it-was chased me
back into the house! I still don't know where Fudgie is!"

"Stay under the truck until this is over," Amanda said
authoritatively. "Fudgie will be fine." She stood up and
adjusted her party clothes, but when she turned again,
she nearly choked!

She was face-to-face with a hideous emerald beast
sporting rows of sharp, slime-dripping teeth. The
monster had a lobster's body and snapping claws beneath
the head of an alligator. It stood upright and glared down
at her menacingly with yellow eyes.

Amanda didn't have time to think. She ran. She ran faster than she had run in her life, and farther, too, hoping that she was drawing the *thing* away from Sh'Shelle.

"Follow me, Greenie," she mumbled, bearing down and running faster still.

Amazingly, Amanda never ran out of breath. As a matter of fact, in the midst of her escape, Amanda actually felt as if she were getting stronger—drawing strength from some hidden wellspring deep inside her. Her arms and legs felt sure and steady; they seemed to be gaining power and urging her on. Gone were the nausea and side stitches she usually experienced during forced runs in gym. Instead she felt, well, exhilarated, like a peak athlete. It was a feeling she hadn't anticipated experiencing in her life. Ever.

On top of that, her breathing was not in the least bit strained. In fact, oxygen seemed to be pouring into her effortlessly. Her head tingled. She felt so . . . so plain different that she closed her eyes for a second. Then came the strangest sensations of all. With her eyes closed, Amanda could still "see." Not like a movie playing in her head. No. Different than that. But it was *like* seeing.

She could feel the heat of the things around her forming shapes. And she recognized moisture, too. And sounds. She could actually "see" sounds through vibration; it was as if she had—

"Sensilla!" she said aloud, still streaking down the road at top speed.

Amanda had dreamed of what it would be like to have the same sensing hairs that insects had. She'd imagined it to be awesome but never quite this intense. She became aware, without turning or slowing, that she had totally outpaced the clawbster. He was no longer behind her. And the amazing thing was, the information was coming to her from her very own forehead!

Amanda slowed to a stop on Belcher Street, near the edge of town. Reaching up, she gently touched one of two long, thin protrusions at her hairline. The extensions were about five inches long, flexible, and incredibly sensitive. They felt electric.

Briefly, Amanda wondered if she had skewered her

forehead when she'd taken that tumble into Emily's buffet. Had there been fondue? *No.* The protrusions weren't some sort of fancy cutlery; they were a part of her. She'd apparently grown them.

"Wow . . . wow. Wow! I have antennae," she said in a whisper. "Antennae!" she shouted at the empty street. It was, for Amanda, a dream *and* a nightmare. She walked closer to the plate-glass window of the local salon, Curl Up and Dye, and peered at her reflection. Antennae were just a part of it. The skin on Amanda's arms and legs had changed, too. It looked normal, maybe a little glossier, but when she ran a hand over her forearm, it felt hard and smooth like a clear shell. Like armor. The new skin also

ANTENNAE

• Antennae are long, thin sensory organs found in pairs on the heads of insects, crustaceans, and some other arthropods.

• Antennae can be used for smelling, hearing, tasting, and touching.

SENSILLA

• Sensilla are small, hairlike sensory organs that detect temperature, humidity, chemicals, light, and motion.

• Sensilla can be found in many areas on an insect's body but are often clustered on or near the antennae.

covered her back and shoulders. She knocked on her chest with a fist and was rewarded with a rapping sound.

Amanda looked around for someone, anyone, to confirm that she was actually seeing what she thought she was seeing, but there wasn't a soul in sight. Cars had been abandoned in the streets. Doors stood open. The green monsters had frightened away everyone.

Almost everyone. The sound of breaking glass made Amanda whirl around. A greasy-looking kid with blond hair was climbing through the window of Game On, a small video-game store, with the devious plan to rob it while the owners were fleeing for their lives.

Why do people have to be like that? Amanda wondered. *What a scumbag!* Without thinking, she zipped over to the store and stared in through the broken window. "What do you think you're doing?" she demanded, hands planted on her hips.

The kid didn't even look up. He was busy shoving stuff into his backpack. "I said, 'WHAT do you think you're DOING?'" Amanda shouted. This time the kid looked, and when he did, Amanda knew she hadn't been

imagining the changes she had seen in the glass at Curl Up. This kid saw them, too.

The boy froze and stuttered, "Sh-sh-shouldn't you b-be g-green . . . and g-g-glowing?"

"Shouldn't *you* be in jail?" Amanda retorted. This punk disgusted her. The town was in trouble and he was stealing stupid video games! Distaste built up inside her until she felt like she might just explode. And then . . . she sort of . . . did. Her pores opened in unison and unleashed her disgust. The full-body burp produced a large musky cloud that fumigated the store and caused the thief to collapse unconscious onto the low-pile carpet.

Amanda cringed. She'd long admired brown marmorated stink bugs and their ingenious defense weapons, but even she had to admit this was a little . . . gross.

Antennae? Body armor? Biochemical . . . weaponry?

"What is going ON?" she screamed into the empty streets.

manda kept yelling as she searched for explanations as to what was happening to her body, and to her town, but the only reply she got was the echo of her own voice. She was alone on the street—everyone else in Oyster Cove had taken cover somewhere. And even the monsters that had frightened the population away seemed to be departing. The hybrid creeps were launching themselves into the air, heading toward a central meeting place.

Okay, then. Amanda adjusted her course. Wherever these booger bullies were going, she was going.

The sky was bright with the monsters' glow. As more of the creatures changed direction and fell in line, they formed blazing green arches that rose up into the sky before curving back down to earth in the distance.

The sheer numbers gave Amanda the willies but did not slow her down. She ran full speed toward the horde, her antennae alerting her that the situation ahead was a matter of life and death. She pushed herself to the maximum. Her feet became a blur.

Finally, in the warehouse district, Amanda skidded to a halt. The monstrosities were touching down in a large empty lot next to the town's grimy power plant. As each one descended, it joined a giant circle of its brethren speeding around something or someone trapped in the center of the ring. Amanda was able to spot two figures caught in the middle of the vortex—two figures who were vastly outnumbered and clearly in trouble!

Amanda moved in slowly, but the swirling beasts paid her no mind. When she was close enough to have a clear view inside the circle, her mouth fell open in disbelief. There at the very center of the spiraling frenzy stood . . .

No. It didn't seem possible.

Amanda squinted. Her enhanced insecto-vision was helping her process the action, but she could not quite believe what she was seeing.

The costumes. The symbols. Those boots! The pair in the center of the monsters' vortex were none other than

Megawoman and Dragonfly!

Amanda nearly cheered out loud. *Of course* Megawoman and Dragonfly were here! In the face of danger, Oyster Cove's own superheroes had returned to save the day. And it appeared they were about to face off against the whole pack of degenerates! Amanda bit her lips together and hoped her slightly rebellious and quickly changing body would not betray her excitement by shooting rainbow mist out of her belly button or something equally startling. She had never dared hope to see her beloved heroes in the flesh—and yet here they were, looking exactly like the action figures she used to build tree-stump houses and create wild adventures for!

Suddenly this nightmare of a day was turning into a dream. And Amanda allowed herself a moment to ponder all that this could mean—the exciting reappearance of Megawoman and Dragonfly in this, Oyster Cove's hour of need, was sure to bring a return of the respect the women deserved. Willikers, it could even mean a whole new line of products—perhaps even a new and improved Dragonfly Super Bus, the action-figure vehicle of Amanda's dreams!

But then, as Amanda neared the heroes, her smile began to wilt. Something was wrong. What were Dragonfly and Megawoman waiting for? They were standing together . . . back to back with looks of grim determination on their faces, like they always did in the show before they started whomping villains, but they weren't moving. Like, at all. Nor were the monsters advancing. . . .

Squinting at them from her spot outside the ring, Amanda noticed something terrible: The überwomen were bound up in some sort of shiny string.

"No!" Amanda heard herself scream. The monsters turned, but she hardly noticed. The heroes turned, and she locked eyes with Dragonfly. A jolt of she-didn't-even-know-what shot through her body.

It was said that with her amazing vision and sight-enhancing drago-mask, Dragonfly could see in every direction at once. Criminals claimed she could "see through them." Amanda instantly understood why. The super-hero's gaze was penetrating. It felt like . . . like . . . she could speak with her eyes. . . . It felt like she *knew* her.

With that glance, Amanda knew she had to do something! She set her jaw and was prepared to break into the monster circle, when a terrible, shattering sound split the air. Dust lifted up in billowing clouds. The heroes were obscured. Amanda heard two cries and then, as the air cleared, her dream was once again a nightmare.

The bound Dragonfly and Megawoman hovered above a large hole in the earth, held aloft by otherworldly armatures that had emerged from the ground. One was wrapped around Megawoman, holding her legs together at the knees and covering her mouth. The weird winding arms were burly, too. Only something with truly amazing strength could squeeze superstrong Dragonfly tightly enough to gag and immobilize her!

"No!" Amanda looked directly at Dragonfly, pleading with her to bust a move. "Do something!"

Dragonfly looked back, and her multifaceted eyes opened wide in a gaze of sad recognition . . . and defeat.

And then Megawoman and Dragonfly were dragged down into the dirt.

Rubble spilled into the strange sinkhole after the captives—and in the time it took for Amanda to gasp, they were gone. Swallowed up. Leaving Amanda gawking.

The pit had disappeared completely. Within seconds, it was covered over with dirt, as if it had never been. Above it, the monsters swirled aimlessly.

"You lowlife bogsuckers!!" Amanda screamed as loudly as she could at the closest green ghoul—an oversize naked mole rat and moray eel combo. Then, without a moment of concern for her personal safety, she hurled herself at the huge beast. She ran full tilt—ready for impact—right *through* the terrifying monster!

"What the—!?" Amanda slid to a stop on the other side of the nasty thing. She looked back. It was still there! She'd passed through it. . . . The green beasts were holograms!

The moment Amanda figured out that they posed no threat, the apparitions began to retreat, swirling rapidly into the sky. Within minutes, they had vanished.

But the hole *had* been there.

And the monsters.

And the heroes.

All that was left was Amanda and her dismay.

Her whole body screamed. The battle was lost. Amanda blinked back tears. She did not want to be brave anymore. She wanted her mom. Now.

Running as fast as she could—which was really amazingly fast with her souped-up insectile features—toward home, Amanda felt like an ant separated from its colony: desperate and alone. A solitary ant was vulnerable without the protection of its community. Severed from its colony, the tiny insect would soldier endlessly on until it found its nest . . . or died trying.

8

The Prices' house was on the inland edge of Oyster Cove in Stubby Oaks, a neighborhood of houses that used to be shacks for seasonal visitors who could not afford to stay on the beach. The home was small and cozy, quiet and quaint, with scroll-cut trim and a front door with a little window in it. As she ran into the yard, Amanda imagined her mom sitting at the kitchen table as she did every day, waiting to hear all about the insect her daughter had rescued on her way home or the amazing fact she'd read in her library book about larvae. She could practically hear her mother's reassuring voice and could not wait for her to say that everything was going to be fine.

Only her mom wasn't there.

The house was quiet.

"Mom!" Amanda called. "Mom!" No Mom.

Amanda shook her head in an attempt to clear her

mind. Good gravy, the thoughts racing inside her usually logical brain were frankly just *too* outrageous to be believed. She wanted to rattle them loose so she could prove they were just her overactive imagination getting the best of her.

But there were two things keeping Amanda from thinking that she'd made up the absurd story. They were the two waving antennae on her forehead. Yes, those appendages currently wiring distress signals to her brain were very, very real. And they would not shut up about the fact that she needed to locate her mother. Like, now.

Taking a deep breath, Amanda tried to think sensibly. She was pretty certain that no matter how relaxing the yoga-pi-latte exercises were, her mom and Emily's would not have lingered at the gym during the whole crazy invasion episode. Like any caring parents, they would have raced home to check on their children—and their children's guests. *Of course*, Amanda thought. *They are at the Battfields'. Yes. They would have rushed back immediately!* Carefully, Amanda dialed the number she still knew by heart.

Emily picked up on the third ring. Her voice sounded oddly hopeful and a little stuffed up.

"Hello?"

"Emily, it's Amanda. Is my mom there?" She wasn't wasting any time.

Emily let out a sigh. "Noooooooo." She drew the single syllable out much longer than necessary to emphasize her distaste at having to speak to Amanda on the phone. Then sniffled.

"Wait," Amanda said, dismissing the girl's tone. "Have you been crying?"

There was a long silence on the other end of the line.

"The party is over," Emily finally huffed. Then she hung up.

"Duh," Amanda whispered.

Insulted, exoskeletal, and alone, Amanda made another call.

Within minutes, Vincent arrived out of breath on Amanda's doorstep. The first words out of his mouth when she opened the door were, "May I try that on?" Vincent's green eyes grew wider behind his plastic frames as he admired Amanda's antennae and exoskeleton. "Do . . . do you think it comes in my size?"

"It doesn't come off," Amanda explained, marveling at how quickly she was growing used to her body's changes. Just thinking of removing her antennae or protective layer for someone else to put on sounded sort of ridiculous—like letting someone try on your face. Of course, she realized, it was a gigantic bummer that her changes appeared to be permanent. There was no way she could be seen at school like this! In fact, that was going to be a huge problem. . . .

But dealing with these "changes" was not what Amanda was freaking out about *currently*. Right at this moment, Amanda was freaking out about her mom—she had to find her ASAP—and she could feel a meltdown rising dangerously close to the surface. "We'll talk about my accessories later," she said, fixing Vincent with a look that made his questions fade into the background. "Right now, we have an emergency."

As quickly as she could, Amanda filled Vincent in on all that had gone on, including the reappearance of and near-immediate redisappearance of the town's heroes, Megawoman and Dragonfly. She knew he loved them, and he listened closely, his eyes growing wider with each new revelation.

"Jeepers! You had an actual *sighting*!" he screeched. "But if Dragonfly and Megawoman have been abducted, we have *got* to call the police!" Grabbing the phone, Vincent thrust it at Amanda and demanded that she dial 9-1-1!

Right. Of course. When a person is snatched, you alert authorities, Amanda thought, soothed by the sensible suggestion. *And I can tell them about my mom, too.*

The authorities would help. They would take over, locate her mom, rescue the heroes, and everything would be fine.

Amanda felt her breathing normalize as she dialed the emergency number. It was busy. She tried again and again until she finally got what sounded like a very harried, not-too-interested voice on the line.

"Hi, my name is Amanda Price, and I have some very important information. You have got to alert everyone that the green things that attacked the town are just holograms. They're not real! Also, I just saw Megawoman and

Dragonfly being kidnapped!" she blurted.

"Sure, kid. A lot of people have been seeing a lot of things tonight. We're getting crazy reports from all over town, and we're working as fast as we can. But I'll be sure to add this to the list," the operator droned, and then let out a guffaw. "Wouldn't it be great, though, if Dragonfly and Megawoman would show up and take care of this? That's some dream. I'm gonna tell that one to the captain."

"But I'm telling the truth!" Amanda shouted. "And there's another emergency, too," she said quickly before the operator could hang up.

Not surprisingly, after listening to the story about her missing mother, the operator informed her that an unexplained absence of less than twenty-four hours did not constitute an emergency, especially given Oyster Cove's current dire situation. The very best advice he had for Amanda was to find a relative to stay with and to call back if her mom was gone longer than forty-eight hours.

"Fiddlesticks!" Amanda fumed, slamming the phone down. "The police aren't going to help at all! But I know my mother. She wouldn't just leave. Something is wrong."

Vincent looked at her sympathetically. "All right. Let's have a sit-down and review the facts. We have to be rational. But first, do you mind if I help myself to a beverage? All this excitement has made me parched!"

Vincent tugged the refrigerator open while Amanda slumped onto the sofa in the living room. She heard a small gasp from the vicinity of the sink.

"Um, Amanda?" Vincent called. When she got to the kitchen, Vincent was leaning on the counter and pointing into the fridge. There, along with the usual selection of healthy vegetable and fruit concoctions, was a note propped against a container of organic hemp milk. The envelope read "Sugar Beet."

"I think we might have a conversation starter for our discussion," Vincent squeaked, plucking up the envelope and handing it to her.

Amanda stared at it for a moment. There, in her mother's handwriting, was one of the many, many pet names she called Amanda on a daily basis. If this note was waiting for her, her mother must have known something was going to happen. . . .

She ripped open the top, pulled out the letter, and began to read aloud.

"Peanut, if you are reading this, it is because I have been detained. Emily's mom and I are planning something this evening we haven't tried in a long time. If we were successful, you would never have known about it. But if we weren't—which is why you're reading this—then you're going to have to be strong now and grow up a little faster than either of us might have wanted.

"I'm so sorry, Sweet Pea, but there are things about me that I've kept from you for reasons you will soon understand."

Amanda turned to Vincent. "Wh-what the heck is going on here?" she stammered.

"Keep reading!" Vincent ordered, pushing the paper toward Amanda's face.

"Please forgive me, Snickerdoodle. I cannot be explicit. For your own safety, and mine, you will need to figure out the following clues. I have faith you can do it quickly. And I know you'll rise to the occasion. It's in your blood. Just be strong, Dumpling, and we'll be together soon, I promise. Now, here are the clues:

Zephyr

13

180

"*Also, give Poppy a call. He's on speed dial #1. He will come right away to stay with you. He's been waiting for this call for a long time, and he can help, I promise.*

"*Love you, Pumpkin. —Mom.*"

Amanda finished reading and stared at the note in disbelief. Her mother had not only left her, but she'd left her a puzzle—a puzzle that their safety depended upon!

9

manda let the paper fall to the ground. She was in shock. Her mother was "detained" (whatever that meant), and Poppy, who had been pretty old and out of it the *last* time she'd seen him (which was several years ago), was supposed to come be her guardian, and she had to figure out some crazy clues.

Dang.

This had been some day.

But given the enormity of the situation, there was nothing for Amanda to do but follow instructions. Vincent handed her the phone—they were on the same page, as usual—and she hit speed dial #1. A cracking voice invited her to leave a message.

"Hi, it's Amanda, your granddaughter. Mom told me to call. She's, uh . . . missing and said you'd be able to help." There. Amanda hung up and threw up her hands.

It was an odd message, but she hoped Poppy would get the point.

Vincent was already bent over the note, looking at the clues. "Zephyr?" he asked.

Zephyr was obvious. At least it was obvious to Amanda. Her mother was a notorious runner—it was a part of her health regimen. She ran every morning along the trail the city had installed from the beach up to the hills. She ran in marathons. She ran half marathons. She ran in her sleep. She also ran on a treadmill in the basement, and she had given the machine a nickname: Zephyr. Her mother had been smart—Zephyr was a name only she and Amanda knew. Every night she joked about visiting Zephyr before sprinting downstairs for her workout.

Now it was Amanda's turn to sprint downstairs. She and Vincent faced Zephyr in its sleek glory in the far corner of the semifinished basement. Next to the treadmill were a television and a small stereo.

"Say, while we're puzzling over that letter, let's turn on the news and see if there are any developments," Vincent suggested. He tuned in to channel 44, WTOC, and the two friends listened as they examined the treadmill. From the sound of it, the attack was over and reporters were getting reactions. None of them pleasant.

"Citizens of Oyster Cove are outraged," Councilman Lester Shrimpfax said into a microphone that had been thrust in his face. "Megawoman and Dragonfly swore to protect us from all elements of evil. They took an oath! Right here in front of this very statue! While it's true we have not needed their help in some time, we needed them tonight, and they were not here!" Shrimpfax glared into the camera while the reporter reminded him of the boatload of good the heroes had already done in years past. "Well . . . but"—the flustered councilman's face took on a nasty bruised hue—"that doesn't excuse them from pitching in when they're needed. Look around! This place is trashed. And these shenanigans had better be taken care of before the Oyster Cove Day celebration or heads will roll!"

Oyster Cove Day. Somehow the town's largest event seemed less important in light of what was happening *now*.

"Why isn't anyone *worried* about the heroes?" Amanda screamed at the TV, still angry that the police hadn't taken her story seriously. "They're in trouble!"

The news report rolled on. "Just look what happened to my date palm," Oyster Cove resident Madge Flimmerman seethed to an on-the-scene reporter. "My lawn's been ruined. Those dames really let us down tonight."

Amanda shook her head. "Typical."

"While no one can be certain where tonight's invaders came from, or even what they were, we are glad to report that there have been no fatalities or serious injuries," the newscaster continued. "The worst that can be reported is severe property damage and a once peaceful evening turned upside down. Stay tuned to WTOC for updates. In the meantime, stay safe."

"Duh. They're holograms." Amanda swallowed her frustration with the townsfolk and refocused her efforts on Zephyr. It wasn't her fault that everyone panicked and the police wouldn't believe her. She had other work to do. Her mother's clues weren't going to solve themselves.

"Vinnie, turn that off and help me," she ordered. Her irritation made the request come out bossier than usual. Luckily, Vincent totally got her.

"Yes, ma'am." He saluted, skipping over to the TV before returning to the mysterious treadmill. The two studied the gadgets on the machine's upper panel. One screen was for counting calories (though her mother told her that one was useless), another was for the level, and yet another was a timer.

Vincent pointed at the one in the middle. "I bet you need to activate this contraption and set it here." He poked at the highest level: thirteen—Olympian Goddess.

"No way! That's the toughest one! No one can do that level," Amanda scoffed. "Especially not me. . . . You've seen me in gym. One lap takes me four weeks."

"Right," Vincent countered. "But that was the *old* you. Didn't you say you were sprinting all up and down this town like a shot?"

"Well, I *was* pretty impressed with myself," Amanda admitted. "I guess I can see if I've still got the juice." Amanda started jogging slowly at first. She had only used Zephyr once before and had gotten off it after three seconds. She'd found the experience boring. Now that her mother's life might depend on her, though, she was less

skeptical about the treadmill's importance.

"It's on five right now," Vincent stated. "I'm going to turn it up to ten." Amanda picked up her pace. After another minute, she gave Vincent the thumbs-up, and he dialed it all the way to Olympian Goddess.

"Thirteen, here we come," Vincent trilled as he worked the panel, taking the treadmill—and Amanda—to speeds she hadn't thought possible. Startled by the velocity, Amanda started to puff a little but quickly realized she was doing just fine. Great, even. This was cake!

"Okay," she breathed. "We've got thirteen down. Now what's the one-eighty?"

"I'm guessing it's seconds," Vincent replied. He was smart, and Amanda trusted him. "Keep going for two more minutes and we'll be up to one-eighty!"

Amanda ran and ran. The seconds ticked by.

178 . . . 179 . . . 180. The magic number!

When she passed the three-minute mark on the treadmill, racing at Olympian Goddess speed, there was a hissing noise, like exhaust from a braking bus, and a dark portal opened in the wall before them.

"Whoa," Vincent gasped. "Supersecret spy stuff!"

Amanda, too taken aback to realize what she was doing, stopped in midrun. The treadmill, still racing at Olympian Goddess, whipped her up into an aerial tumble. She hit the back wall and crashed down with a thud.

"Oof." The air rushed out of her, and she gave a rap on her hip. "Well, at least we know this hard shell is protective. I barely felt a thing!" Standing up, she dusted herself off a bit. And then she shuddered.

A secret entrance to a secret something loomed before her. A something her mother had never dared tell her about before, or even hint at. Her mother ran, had jars with various bean sprouts lining her kitchen windowsills, made her own tofu, ate lots of fiber, and refused to buy water in plastic bottles. She was a fitness freak and a hippie! What could be lurking beyond this ominous doorway?

There was only one way to find out.

"You're coming with me," Amanda ordered her friend.

"You're darn right I am," he snapped back. "You think I'd miss out on this? Let's go. You first."

Amanda shrugged. Of course she would go first. After

all, she was the one with the newfangled protective gear. Plus, it was *her* mom—and her mom's secret.

The two crept down into the darkness, feeling their way slowly and carefully along a steep staircase, until they noticed a red glow ahead. The light grew more intense as they descended until at last they were standing on flat ground. Amanda could see that the glow was coming from some sort of computer.

"A light switch!" Vincent called, after fumbling along the walls for a moment. "Brace yourself, I'm turning it on!"

The fluorescent overhead flickered on as Amanda and Vincent gazed in wonder at some sort of high-tech communications center lining the far wall of the large room.

"Whoa!" Vincent called, after turning to his right. "Amanda, your mom isn't just missing. . . ."

Amanda turned to see what Vincent was talking about. What she saw rendered her speechless.

"She's been kidnapped," her friend added.

Displayed on the side wall was an impressive collection of newspaper articles, awards, banners, photographs, and in the center, a tall Plexiglas case. Resting within that case was a pristine costume that belonged to the world-famous Dragonfly. Its green and black fabrics shimmered in the obnoxious lighting with the same majestic sparkles that must have shone when the hero was still battling bad guys. The cape was short, its gold lamé exterior complemented by a deep-red metallic lining. The mask was a glittering onyx that covered the nose and eyes. It was beautiful. And what it meant was incredible.

"Your mom . . . she's Dragonfly . . . and that makes you . . . Oyster Cove royalty!" Vincent sputtered, unable to contain himself. "I'm going to need a minute."

"You and me both," Amanda said, shaking her head.

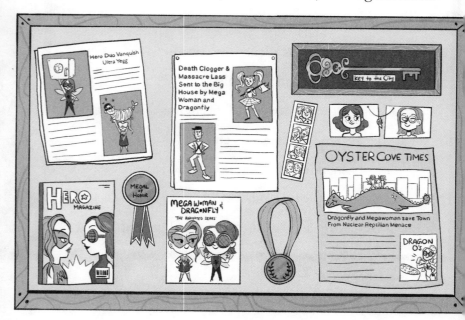

She was in shock. She knew her mom was pretty fit, *but*... this was harder to believe than sprouting antennae! And yet believing it made so many other things make sense (like, for example, the sprouting antennae).

frozen yogurt after defeating Sinister Sally

Amanda stared at the wall, absorbing as much as she could. Newspaper clippings boasted of Megawoman and Dragonfly's heroic exploits.

Amanda examined everything closely. Mixed in with the articles and swirling psychedelic decor were photos of Dragonfly and Megawoman when they were young. She squinted at Dragonfly. She'd never noticed the resemblance before, but confronted with the evidence, it was clear. Dragonfly was definitely her mother. And Megawoman . . . was also oddly familiar. "Vincent, look! It's Emily's mom. Mrs. Battfield is Megawoman!"

Vincent was practically vibrating with amazement. In a minute Amanda was going to have to fetch him a cold compress to dab on his temples if he didn't calm down.

Amanda was feeling a little dizzy herself. Dragonfly

and Megawoman. Her mom and Emily's. The two were close friends, and had been for, well, forever. And now, looking at all this, Amanda realized exactly why her mother had been so insistent about Emily. If Amanda was destined to follow in her mother's footsteps—and this hard shell she'd grown, along with her new ability to stop thieves in their tracks using buglike powers, made it seem like she was—then it made sense that Emily would be carrying on her own mother's legacy. Which meant that Amanda would probably be doomed not only to talk to but also *work* with Emily for the rest of her life. With a sigh, Amanda decided to think about that situation later. Because before she could contemplate any sort of future, she had to find (and rescue) her mom.

With renewed resolve, Amanda began a thorough search of the lair while Vincent marveled over the intricacies of Dragonfly's costume. "Look at this stitching!" he burbled, but Amanda really didn't have time for that. Her mother had said she was attempting something. She had known something was going to happen. Something big enough to get her to reveal her secret. Something big

enough to get her pulled underground.

The central computer at Amanda's mother's workstation was on but in sleep mode. When she tapped the keyboard, the computer woke up.

"Greetings, Dragonfly," the computer droned. "Initiate retina scan."

"Lean in!" Vincent said. "It wants to scan your eyeball. You know, to make sure you're authentic."

"Okay, here goes," Amanda said tentatively. She leaned in, and a red beam scanned her face once and then twice. The computer blinked and thought for a moment, and then announced that for security purposes, it would be shutting down. The machine warned that if anyone other than Dragonfly made a second attempt to access information, it would self-destruct.

"Cripes, I blew it," Amanda said. "Now what?"

"No pouting," Vincent said, wagging a finger. "We've got plenty to go on. Let's just find another place to start."

Shelves stuffed with file folders that looked similar to a doctor's medical charts flanked the desk. Opening a few, Amanda discovered that each was dedicated to a particular villain or case, and they were overflowing with clippings, photos, data sheets, and police reports. Her mom was not messing around.

Then Amanda saw a pile of folders stacked on the desk, ready for business. On top of them was a sticky note that read *Here we go again. Top suspects.* Along with a recipe for a spirulina shake. It also had a date—yesterday's. Amanda scanned the labels: Calamity Coven; Porcine Sisters; Dark Tarsier; and The Exterminator—a baddie so awful he boasted a folder thicker than a grilled-cheese sandwich with triple cheddar.

Amanda drew a mental picture of a tireless dung beetle. The shiny bugs worked ceaselessly, *backward and upside down,* to cut and sculpt and roll life-sustaining balls of nastiness three times their size to their burrows, fighting off competitors all along the way. Those little beetles just put their heads down and kept rolling. And that was what Amanda needed to do now, too.

DUNG BEETLE

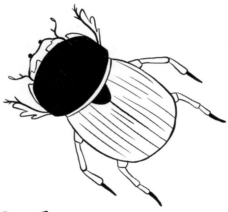

Fun Bug Fact: Dung beetles can push around poop balls that are more than fifty times their own weight. Dung beetles have specific tastes—different species have different preferences as to which poop they eat, and they like their food fresh. They also use the stars to navigate.

I t was nearly morning when a soft knock on the door startled Amanda awake. She hadn't gone to bed—the day had been too strange for her to feel right about doing anything as normal as crawling into her pajamas and cuddling under the covers—but she had dozed off on the couch once she'd sent Vincent home. She blinked slowly and gave a big yawn as she staggered toward the soft but insistent knocking. She was exhausted.

Rubbing her eyes, Amanda noted that her skin had returned to normal (thank goodness). She wasn't sure how or why that had happened, or if her nifty coating would come back, but she'd have to think about that later. Groggy, she opened the door and stared at the old man standing on her stoop.

The slightly hunched man spread his arms and wrapped her in an awkward hug.

"Mandy, don't you remember your old Poppy?" he asked when she shrugged out of the hold.

"Poppy?" Amanda rubbed her eyes some more. She had not seen her grandfather in several years, and the version standing before her did not exactly match the one in her memory.

"I'm here to take care of you," Poppy exclaimed, clapping his hands together. Amanda realized she was glad he had arrived. It was nice not to be alone, and she was going to need as much help as she could get. Relieved and more awake, Amanda gave her grandfather a proper hug and led him into the house.

"Poppy, have you seen the news?" Amanda asked, peering outside. The coast was still clear of any of those . . . things.

"Yes, I read all the scuttlebutt. Oyster Cove's seeing a bit

grizzled chin

beet juice stain

nimble fingers

timeless fashion sense

attractive orthopedic shoes (rare)

of action," he huffed. "Just like old times, I'd say!"

"Right. That. So what are we going to do about it? No one believes me when I ask for help!" Amanda waited for some major pearls of wisdom to slip from her grandfather's mouth. He must know what to do; otherwise her mother wouldn't have instructed her to call him.

"We'll get to all that in a minute, don't you fret." Poppy smiled, then yawned widely. His chin was dusted with stubbly whiskers, making him look a little like a wet plum that had been dropped in white sand. "Is it lunchtime yet? I'm peckish. Let's eat and then we'll talk about this situation your mother's got herself into."

Amanda looked at the clock. It was almost five A.M. It was definitely *not* lunchtime. "I can make you an egg?" she offered.

"Can't stand 'em. I'll have two. Poached. That is, if you don't have any pasta in the house. Got noodles?"

Amanda hurried to the kitchen and put a small pot of water on the stove. She checked the cupboard for dried pasta, but her mother tried to avoid white flour, so all she found was a mess of quinoa.

Waiting for the water to boil for eggs, Amanda stared out the window and wondered if she might be dreaming. The early hour added to the surreal quality of the situation. Outside, not even the fireflies were flickering.

When Amanda went back into the living room carrying two poached eggs on gluten-free toast and a cup of tea, she found that Poppy had dozed off. But clearly he was not something she'd cooked up in Slumberland. He was real, and he was really there.

"Ehr-hehrm." Amanda cleared her throat so his snack wouldn't get cold. Poppy jerked upright. "Where's your mother?" he asked loudly. He looked around the room. Apparently the micronap had perked him up.

"Oh. Right, right. You don't know," Poppy said, before launching into some epic mumbling. "Probably some heroic theatrics. That girl. Always sticking her neck out. She told me she was done with all that, but I knew better. I should have been here. Never should have moved to Florida. People there drive slow, you know."

Poppy was rambling to himself, but it was obvious that he knew more about her mother's secret life than Amanda did. And he seemed to be taking her mother's disappearance in stride—how, she was not sure. Just thinking about the situation again was making Amanda panic.

Amanda's pulse quickened, and her antennae began to emerge involuntarily. Her skin started to take on the sheen it'd had before. She was changing! Feeling a little shy, she turned to flee as Poppy put his fork into the yolk of his early-morning nosh, scooped it up, and froze. He held the bite aloft for a moment before putting it in his mouth.

"Hold up there, missy. I don't know if it's a good idea to flaunt what you got going on there around town." Poppy waved his fork in circles, flinging yolk. "You best keep that hidden."

"I'd like to, but . . ." Amanda squeezed her eyes shut. She could not believe she was talking about her . . . bug stuff . . . with her grandpa! She tried her hardest to calm her antennae, but the more she tried to make them retract, the more they continued to grow. "I can't!"

"Take a breath, Mandy," Poppy instructed, lazily chewing. "Now think about spaghetti."

Amanda frowned. How could she think about food

when she was mutating in front of her grandfather? Talk about awkward. But just *thinking* about thinking about spaghetti seemed to do . . . something. Her feelers began to withdraw. She chanted the names of every type of pasta she could think of under her breath.

"Capellini, rigatoni, fettuccini, macaroni . . ."

And watched in the mirror over the fireplace as her antennae retracted entirely. The macaroni meditation made her skin go back to normal. Poppy was on to something!

The old man nodded and returned to his snack.

"Poppy?" Amanda asked cautiously. "About Mom . . . Have you ever been in our basement?"

"So, you've found the lair, huh?" Poppy wheezed. "Of course I've been in that basement! I helped your ma build it back when she was just a spring chicken. Took a lot of work, too. You try finding a supercomputer around these parts that can tap into the world's crime-fighting networks, and see how easy it is!" He waved his fork again, flinging more yolk onto the floor.

"It's a good thing I'm here," he continued, losing interest in his eggs. "You, missy, are going to need help just like your ma did. We'll get you set up right, don't you worry. How about we start with you telling me about those deely-boppers on top of your head?"

"*This* stuff just started yesterday," Amanda explained, looking anywhere but at Poppy. "It comes on all of a sudden. Like when I'm scared or nervous. My skin turns hard, and I can run really fast, and . . . those things . . ." Amanda stopped there. She wasn't ready to talk biochemical emissions with Poppy just yet. "And I guess when I calm down it all goes away."

"Mm-hmm." Poppy nodded, slowly chewing. "You take after your ma, all right—bug stuff. But like I said, you best stuff that business under your hat. Your mother was careful to keep you out of her dealings for a reason."

"But how am I supposed to keep my bug stuff a secret when it just . . . pops up? Just think about noodles all the time?" Even if noodle thoughts worked in her living room, it was clear that fear (and even just anxiety) made her insectness appear whether she wanted it to or not. "There is no way I can go back to school," she said out loud.

"Of course you can. And you will," Poppy announced. "It's going to be business as usual around here. We shall carry on like nothing has happened."

Yeah, nothing except I'm part bug and my superhero mom's been hijacked and my grandfather may not be the freshest egg in the basket, Amanda thought.

"Now you go try and get some rest," Poppy ordered. "You'll need it! We'll discuss these shenanigans later. And don't you worry your little head. Compared to some of the messes your mother and I've been through, this is a walk in the park. You'll see! Giddyap on out of here and get to bed."

Amanda didn't think she would be able to sleep at all, but she shuffled reluctantly to her room. As the sun was rising, she finally drifted off—but her slumber was fitful and filled with nightmare images. She tossed and turned, watching horrors playing out in her head, the worst of which left her spooked and sweaty: a vision of her mother rendered moth-size, flying closer and closer to one of those awful blue porch zappers.

11

Amanda's nightmares finally faded, and she fell into a deep sleep. When she woke, she was surprised to discover that it was dark outside. Of course she'd been exhausted, but she'd never expected that she'd be able to sleep through an entire day. Certainly not at a time like this! She must really have needed it. She looked at her clock. It read 7:15. There was no more time to lose.

Amanda padded barefoot into the living room to find Poppy reading the newspaper and looking right at home.

"Quite the show the other night, I see," he commented. He held up the newspaper. There, front and center, was a giant beast harassing pedestrians downtown.

"More like a horror movie," Amanda said, rubbing sleep from her eyes.

"So these are the guys that took your ma and her trendy pal?" Poppy poked a gnarled finger at the picture.

"No . . ." Amanda was unclear about who or what had *actually* taken them. The greenies had lured them, that was for sure. But then the hole . . . and the arms . . . "Those booger things weren't even real. I mean, they had no substance. I actually passed right through one!" she boasted. "Something else . . . something horrible got my mom. All those green hologram things just took off after the sinkhole opened."

"Took off, huh?" Poppy repeated, sounding a little less surprised than Amanda would have expected. "Sounds like there's more to this business than meets the eye. My guess is you'll be able to get to the bottom of it. Just like your mother used to back in her day. She was quite the feisty one, you know—didn't put up with any arkymalarkey."

Mom. Amanda gulped. She had about a billion questions about her mom, questions she wanted to ask her mother in person.

"So, Poppy, when did my mom find out she was . . . different?" Amanda hoped Poppy would give her a direct answer. She couldn't quite understand how he could be so laid-back about everything. He acted like her mother being swallowed alive was an everyday occurrence. And then she realized, maybe at one time it had been.

"Your ma's always been a little special," Poppy started, "buzzing after bad guys since she was a whippersnapper. That gal just couldn't be stopped. But it wasn't until she and that partner of hers met in college that things got more . . . interesting." Poppy hunkered down to tell a long tale, fussing with the newspaper all the while. And Amanda sank into the couch to listen. "Your ma and that pal of hers were roommates their freshman year. Best friends from the start. And it didn't take long before they learned they had more in common than attending rallies and going to concerts."

Poppy smoothed several sheets of paper onto the divan. "The day they discovered each other's secret abilities was the day a villain known as the Cowboy of Doom came hootin' and hollerin' onto campus. That creepy cowherd rode in mounted on a robotic horse and wearing a dusty blue hat. Then, while everyone stared at his BeDazzled boots, the nasty redneck threatened to round up all the students who were attending the college's Annual Ham Toss and Cotillion! He was apparently mad and bent on revenge, and after raising a ruckus, he corralled a bunch of students on the Ham Runway."

Amanda was rapt. Poppy began folding as he talked.

"Just when it looked like there was no hope of completing the Ham Toss, not one but TWO costumed heroes rushed in to save the day and the game. While one hog-tied the cowpoke—that'd be your ma—the other released the trapped students," Poppy finished, satisfied.

"And the Ham Toss was saved!" Amanda exclaimed, guessing at the happy ending.

"That's right." Poppy nodded. "And before the pork flew or the dust settled, our two heroes decided to team up. When they found a private moment to reveal their secret identities to each other, they laughed to beat the band. They just knew it was destiny that made them best friends and fighting partners—and that their mission was to keep Oyster Cove free of evil and chaos." Poppy smiled with evident pride and blew a puff of air into his intricately folded paper. It inflated into the shape of a frog.

"Your ma and her partner did every little thing together for many years. They were unstoppable," Poppy continued while Amanda sat in awed silence. "They graduated college. They took down a crime syndicate or two. They got married in a double ceremony. They even ushered in the 'Great Time of Peace.' Then they both got pregnant. Soon as they were in the family way, those gals saw things a little differently," Poppy explained.

When the new mothers decided to start raising babies, they had to make some serious decisions. They made a pact and decided to "retire." But only after they'd vanquished all known villains.

"They didn't want to leave any loose ends," Poppy said with a nod.

Amanda was silent a moment longer. Poppy's story explained a whole lot about how and why her granola mama and Emily's sequin-encrusted mother were best friends. And made her worry even more about how hard they'd pushed to keep their daughters together.

"So, Mom and Mrs. Battfield weren't planning to come back, you know, as their superselves? Ever?" Amanda asked. She thought retiring from such an exciting job might have been hard. Her mom always said becoming a mother was the best thing she ever did—but was she comparing that with protecting a community? Vanquishing evil? Saving the world?

"Oh, I don't know if that was the plan." Poppy chuckled to himself and began folding the newspaper into hats.

"Was she ever going to tell me?" Amanda asked.

"I think she planned to tell you one day. When you were ready," Poppy said, trying on one of the hats. It was rather piratey, so he tore himself an eye patch and began hobbling around the room with one lip curled.

Amanda ignored him while she processed it all. For

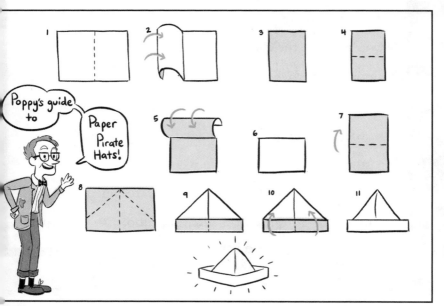

as long as she'd been alive, peace and tranquillity had prevailed in her sleepy town. She supposed that the heroes' reputation alone had been enough to stave off danger after they ceased active duty. She and Emily had known nothing of giant monsters or sinister scoundrels with mad plots growing up—just picnics and trips to the beach and lazy summer vacations.

"This swashbuckling garb needs a little something. . . . Ah! A parrot!" Poppy hooted to himself.

"But, Poppy," Amanda said, to keep him focused, "how did Mom know this was going to happen? She was all dressed and ready."

"Oh, yes. Your ma called to warn me that something was up," Poppy said apologetically. "Said they'd gotten word through the Global Hero Network about some anonymous lunatic who was boasting about 'seeking revenge' and attacking Oyster Cove, blah, blah, blah. But I wasn't worried. I figured she could handle it. But . . . maybe she's rustier than I realized."

Amanda swallowed hard. Poppy resumed walking around the room with a lurching limp, like he had a wooden leg. When he saw the stricken look on Amanda's face, he stopped.

"Don't get your knickers in a knot, Mandy. She'll be back. She always comes back. Now, about that parrot?"

"But, Poppy, what about you?" Amanda asked, scooting forward a little. "You said you helped her."

"Oh, I helped, all right." Poppy chuckled. "When your ma told me about her new partner, I gave her my blessing. But I also told her I'd be her backup. Her behind-the-scenes guy. Every hero needs one of those. We started with that secret room downstairs. Then I helped her come up with some fancy training routines to get her powers in tip-top shape—obstacle courses and such. Can't have a hero going into battle if she can't dodge a laser blast or two. . . ." Poppy paused for effect.

"And whenever your ma went out on her adventures, or missions or what have you, I'd be plunked right down in front of Betsy—that's my nickname for that souped-up computer of hers—and I'd give your ma updated information via earpiece thingamajigs. Keep her up to speed, you understand. One step ahead of the competition."

Amanda gazed at her Poppy with new eyes. He was cool as a cucumber. She was about to ask him how he stayed so calm (was it the pasta thing?) when everything began to shake the same way it had the evening before.

Panic took over. "This is how it started last night!" Amanda shouted. In a split second her antennae were exposed and radioing emergency messages to her skin to armor up.

Poppy put the newspaper crafts down as sirens started to blare outside. "Why, those alarms haven't been in action since World War Two!" He slapped his knee and shuffled to the window like a kid who'd heard the ice cream truck. It was the fastest Amanda had seen him move since he'd arrived.

She raced to the window and stood next to him, both of them peering out into the darkness. Within minutes, searchlights crisscrossed the sky. The sirens continued their plaintive wails. Helicopters appeared overhead, beaming floodlights onto the streets below. And then the green ghouls materialized.

The beasts flooded the streets, looking for pedestrians

to pursue. They swirled into backyards and around cars, searching for anyone out in the open.

"Why are they back? Didn't they get what they came for?" Amanda was a little embarrassed to hear the whine in her voice. "There's not even anybody out there!"

It was true. The sidewalks in Stubby Oaks were abandoned. A lone dog barked frantically at one of the creeps, but the monster paid the animal no mind.

"Maybe that's why," Poppy mused. "It's all flim-flammery. Barnyard glitter. The old razzle-dazzle."

Amanda gave her grandfather a look out of the corner of her eye. She was ready to take back that "cool as a cucumber" thing. More like dotty as a Dalmatian . . .

"My guess," Poppy postulated, "is that we're gonna see a lot more of this. It's a distraction technique, so we don't notice what else is going on. Something bigger is brewing, Mandy, and I bet it's a whopper."

Just then a horseshoe crab and rhinoceros combo swooped close to the window. Amanda shuddered. Her antennae twitched. She knew the monsters weren't solid, but they sure were ugly.

The same urgent drive she'd felt on Saturday welled up inside her until Amanda could not stand it any longer. "Poppy, I've got to go do something about this!" she shouted. She wasn't sure *what* she could do, exactly, but she felt irresistibly drawn into the action. With her antennae extended and her carapace glistening, she started toward the door.

"Hold it right there, Miss Whippersnapper," Poppy called after her.

Amanda stopped.

"Your mother can take care of herself for a skinny minute. We've got work to do."

"But, Poppy, I need to help! Isn't that what being a hero is all about?" Amanda stomped, rattling her mother's crockery collection. She wasn't usually pouty, but *COME ON!*

"Being a hero is about lots of things. We'll start with these." Poppy looked around, bewildered, for a moment and then unfolded one of the paper hats. "Ah, here! We'll start from square one, just like I did with your ma. Wrote this up last night."

On the back of the funnies he had scrawled a list.

1. *Powers*
2. *Instincts*
3. *Skills*
4. *Outfit*
5. *Secret Identity*
6. *Partner*

"Until you've got these things sorted out, you're of no use to anyone. You're just a kid with fancy headgear."

"But"—Amanda plopped down on the couch—"there's not enough time. How am I going to acquire all those things, and . . ." Amanda let her voice trail off. It was hard to admit, but she knew Poppy was right. She couldn't race into this blindly. She needed to train, get outfitted, figure out exactly what she could do, and how. . . .

And she needed to do something else that was going to be even harder: persuade Emily to help.

12

Oyster Cove Middle School sat splat in the middle of town on a hill so small it had to be referred to as a hillock and made Amanda wonder why they didn't just bulldoze it before they started building. Out in front of the big brick rectangle was a statue of a man wearing buckle shoes and a silly hat. Nobody ever bothered to read the placard he stood upon, which declared Tad Parsnippity the founder of the school. Nobody was particularly grateful that the school had been founded.

This morning Amanda was decidedly more ungrateful than usual for the school's existence. She'd spent most of the night "training" with Poppy, doing calisthenics, running wind sprints, and climbing onto the roof of the house so she could practice her jumping. Her skills were coming along, but since she'd gotten just three hours of sleep, her eyelids felt as if they had been sanded, her head pounded,

and gravity was working overtime to pull her toward the center of the planet. Each step was a chore.

Then there was her outfit.

Though she had tried to convince Poppy that macaroni meditations would be effective enough to control her bugginess on campus, Poppy had insisted, and Amanda had been forced to take . . . precautions.

First, in spite of the warm weather, Amanda had pulled on a wool turtleneck and pants. Next she'd located a trench coat, which provided extra coverage and had deep pockets to hide her hands. To top it off, she'd wrapped a scarf around her head several times and prayed it would be enough to contain her antennae should she become agitated.

She was hot, and combined with the worry swirling in her stomach, she felt slightly nauseated as she walked up the school steps.

Luckily the second appearance of the green holograms had everyone talking distractedly, and Amanda, despite her ensemble, was able to walk to her locker without a fuss. Along the way she listened in on the whispers and exclamations of her schoolmates. Judging from the snippets, it seemed everyone was up in arms.

"My dad says it's the end of the world!" LaDonna Tartenhaufer proclaimed. "He read all about it in the *National Inquisitor.*" She poked at the daily rag clutched in her fist. "I brought a copy in to share at circle time!"

"Turkey, please. This is not permanent," Eugenia Thrackmorten spat at the trembling conspiracy theorist. "This is an assault. We are under attack, and there isn't anyone around to rescue us!"

Darren Dibbles joined in the complaining. "Right? Megawoman and Dragonfly are so totally responsible for the town, you know? And they, like, abandoned us!"

"My dad says that Oyster Cove Day might be canceled." Cesar Horowitz nodded, fighting back tears. "My whole year will be ruined if I can't compete in the deviled-egg-eating contest!"

"Maybe Dragonfly and Megawoman were busy?" Missy Simpkin suggested, tentatively defending the town's heroes. "Or they moved away?"

"Those superladies are *long* gone," Justice Herbert sneered. "I bet they'd be old and useless now anyway."

"I heard on the news this morning that the mayor's office received something called a fax, whatever that is, stating that our entire town is getting what's coming to it in just a few days, and that no one, especially Dragonfly and Megawoman, will be here to help us," Mookie Pistachioso chimed in. "It didn't say who the message was from, but it sounds pretty bad."

Amanda's stomach churned faster. She didn't know what a fax was, either, but Mookie's words echoed in her head. *In just a few days . . . no one to help us . . .* someone sending threatening *faxes* to the mayor himself . . . the town heroes could not help. . . . Amanda felt herself being torn in two. Poppy had told her to be patient, but she wasn't sure how long she could handle that!

As she scuttled over to locker 512, she heard another student, Babs Hedgepeth, laugh in Mookie's face. "That's just some silly prank," she said. "This whole messed-up business is just somebody's idea of a joke."

Amanda wasn't laughing. She peeked around the upturned collar of her enormous coat while she worked her locker combo and wished the out-of-date jacket didn't have such massive shoulder pads. She also wished that Vincent and the rest of the Oyster Cove Entomological Society would get to school soon. She hoped her friends would help keep her calm.

Finally, as the first wave of students headed to their homerooms, Amanda's associates slipped nervously through the throng.

"So what did you make of the recent, um, occurrences?" Amanda asked, anxious to hear their take.

"Paranormal activity," Stuart Rigby quickly asserted. "The likes of which haven't been seen since the Great Haunting of '06. Really bad news."

Amanda stepped back. Stuart was a ghost hunter, but really?

"Refractions caused by a meteor shower, obviously," Sylvia Blatherthwaite said skeptically. She researched

everything to death. Astronomy was her favorite. "What did *you* make of them?"

Amanda motioned the geeks to come in closer. "I'm not sure," she said. "But I don't think it was a natural or paranormal phenomenon, and we need to prepare ourselves. The apparitions swarming the town are nothing—there's a more sinister plot afoot. Somebody's threatening the whole town. And things are going to get a lot worse!"

Sylvia snorted and immediately began to cough. Stuart patted her back.

"You're overreacting. Who would threaten Oyster Cove? We don't get that sort of criminal activity here," Sylvia said, pooh-poohing the proposition. "Not anymore. And if we did, I'm sure Megawoman and Dragonfly would buzz back from their tropical island or whatever. It's going to be fine."

Amanda wanted to tell them it wasn't going to be fine. Megawoman and Dragonfly weren't on any tropical island! They had already been captured.

Vincent, who had only just arrived, stood outside the group and took a puff from his inhaler. He held in his breath and, after eyeing Amanda's dreadful outfit with a sour expression, gave her a supportive nod.

Amanda's forehead tingled—she was getting over-emotional.

"I just hope things go back to normal soon," Clementine Varicose sniffled.

Normal. Right. Unfortunately, there was nothing normal about what was happening under Amanda's headscarf. Her skin was crawling. The protective exoskeleton armor had been triggered, and her feelers were twitching like crazy. She considered unwrapping her scarf and revealing her augmentations to shake up her science-minded friends, but Poppy had reminded her over and over while she trained that revealing her strength too soon would make her a target, and a secret identity would only keep her safe if it stayed secret. She could resist the urge.

She thought of penne instead.

By reciting silent noodle incantations and sticking close to Vincent, Amanda made it through most of the morning. Between classes, she scanned the student body nervously, but it wasn't until the lunch bell rang that she spotted Emily.

The blonde was coming down the hall, flipping her hair and pretending to ignore the people flocking around her. Typical. She was acting like nothing had happened.

Amanda took a deep breath.

The mere thought of approaching Emily was enough to make Amanda's skin itch and her antennae tingle painfully beneath the scarf. *Ravioli, ditalini, orecchiette, tortellini.* She steeled herself and called out, "Emily!" Emily didn't bother to look.

"Emily!" Amanda called louder. Nothing. *So rude.*

"EMILY!" Amanda practically screamed. That did it. Emily whirled on her heel. She fixed Amanda with a look and pointed toward the custodial closet.

Amanda knew what she meant. Emily would not talk to her, a social reject, where they would be *seen* conversing. Not when it was Amanda's idea.

Feeling every bit as doomed as a ladybug straying too close to a trapdoor spider's deadfall, Amanda stepped into the closet.

TRAPDOOR
SPIDER

Fun Bug Fact: The trapdoor spider sets a
trap with a silk hinge on one side of a door made
out of mud, silk, and plants. Then it hides under
the door and waits for prey! Watch out!

13

Emily tried to make it look like her closet detour was planned and that she had some urgent janitorial business. But Amanda thought the way she stormed toward the closet with heaving stomps that echoed down the hall brought more attention to the situation than if she had just acted calm. Amanda was aware she had broken the Number One Rule of middle school etiquette imposed upon her by the school's self-imposed ruler: She had called Emily by name. In public.

But it had gotten her attention.

"What?" Emily demanded, slamming the door shut as soon as she had slipped inside. But before Amanda could explain, Emily's eyes adjusted to the low light, and she recoiled. "Holy crab apple. I cannot believe I'm in here. You know I hate low-quality cleaning products," she snorted. "Gross."

RULES OF MIDDLE SCHOOL!!

1. <u>Don't</u> talk to anyone not in your social group.
2. <u>Don't</u> look at anyone not in your social group.
3. <u>Don't</u> breathe near popular people if you are not also a popular person.
4. <u>Don't</u> carry a lunch box.
5. <u>Don't</u> care.
6. <u>Don't</u> even try to become a popular person if you are not a popular person, because it will never work.
7. <u>Don't</u> stand out.
8. <u>Don't</u> blend in.
9. <u>Don't</u> try.
10. <u>Don't</u> wear matching separates.
11. <u>Don't</u> do anything ever.
12. <u>JUST DON'T.</u>

Amanda tried to speak, but Emily was on a roll.

"Plus the moisture in this tacky closet is going to ruin my outfit," she groaned, and began brushing invisible filth off her skirt, as if the act of walking in had caked her in grime. "And furthermore, *why* are you talking to me at school? Did your mom put you up to this?"

"Uh. No. But this *is* about our moms," Amanda said, talking fast. She wasn't sure how much time she had. "Listen, Emily. Something weird is happening, and there are things we need to discuss, like why your mom didn't come home Saturday night." Amanda paused. She looked at Emily, waiting for a reaction.

"What do you mean?" Emily asked. She sounded defensive and a little freaked out. "What are you even talking about?" she asked more slowly, trying to play it off. Amanda saw her response for what it was—an act.

The blonde was as freaked out as she was, if not more—at least Amanda had a clue about what was going on and why her mom hadn't come home. Emily was probably still in the dark. She was probably scared. But even in the dim closet light, Amanda could see that Emily's expression wasn't frightened. Nope. She was radiating pure anger.

"I don't see that that's any of your business," Emily said through tight lips. "But if you must know, my mother is *not* at home. And I'm glad. If she *had* come home Saturday, she would have seen what you did to our living room! Do you know how hard it is to get chocolate out of shag? Lucky for you, Mom left before the party was over. She left . . . on a . . . on a cruise."

A cruise. Oh, please. Amanda knew that Mrs. Battfield despised cruises—the one time they'd all gone on one together, they had vowed never to go again.

With her mother missing, Emily was all by herself—her father had gone away six months earlier because he needed "alone time," as Amanda's mother had diplomatically put it. And he hadn't been in contact since. In other words, the Battfields were breaking up. No doubt the split was hitting Emily hard. Now, with both parents gone, Emily had only Frida to take care of her—though Amanda had always found Frida to be the most levelheaded and capable person in the Battfield house.

"Listen." Amanda reached out and touched Emily's hand. "When our moms left the party, they said they were going to work out. But—"

"No!" Emily yanked her hand back and looked away. She lifted her pert nose a little higher. "I will not listen to another word until you apologize for ruining my party!"

Amanda recoiled from the verbal slap. "Are you kidding?" She blinked. "I'm trying to tell you I think our moms are in troub—Never mind." Amanda stopped talking. There was no point.

Emily had her manicured nails jammed in her ears and was chanting in singsong, "That doesn't sound like an ap-o-lo-gy!"

"Urgh!" Amanda's trapped antennae were really start-

ing to hurt, and she wanted to yank Emily's hands away from her head. *Rotini, tagliatelle, spiralini, pappardelle.* She struggled to keep it together. Losing her temper wasn't going to get her anywhere.

Amanda took a deep breath and started again. "Listen to me! Our mothers are more than just best friends. They're partners. They're crime fighters. My mom is—"

Emily sang louder.

"Emily, are you five? I mean, you're acting like a total kindergartner right now," Amanda finally snapped, loud enough for Emily to hear it. That brought Emily out of her tantrum. She glared at Amanda.

Then, without a word, Emily grabbed the first thing she could get her hands on—a stinky mop that had been hanging on the wall—and snapped it in half. She tossed the broken pieces aside without breaking eye contact.

"Wow," Amanda said, staring down at the splinters. "It's happening to you, too. You're getting powers!"

"Okay, I'm so over this," Emily finally spoke. "Nothing is *happening* to me." She whirled and, with a twist of the handle, was free of the janitorial supply space and back in the crowded halls.

Amanda trotted after her. She had more to say, and Emily needed to hear it!

"Your mother didn't come home because she's Megawoman!" Amanda hissed in Emily's ear. "And she's been kidnapped. And we have to save her!"

Emily tried to wave Amanda off as if she were an annoying gnat. She picked up speed, but Amanda kept pace.

The two girls rounded the corner at a good clip and, *wham*, Emily slammed right into Vincent. The dainty boy was pitched against the lockers. The jolt launched all the data he'd gathered for the Future Scientists Kiosk from his hands and sent it fluttering all over the halls.

"Oof," Vincent huffed as papers rained down around him. He gasped for breath and flattened himself against the lockers to allow Emily to pass.

Amanda stopped. "Oh, Vincent, are you okay?" Vincent could only nod, and Amanda let him steady himself on her arm. Emily continued on her way.

"You can't ignore this! THE MAYOR RECEIVED A

FAX!" Amanda screamed after Emily, still unsure what a fax was. It sounded important, though. "We only have a few days!" she shrieked.

Emily wasn't impressed and continued stomping down the hall. Amanda watched her go, shaking her head. This whole partner thing was *never* going to work.

Halfway down the locker bank, Emily turned, just for a second, and looked back at Amanda and Vincent. Amanda looked into her eyes. There was something there that reminded Amanda of her eighth birthday party—when Amanda had gotten the Megawoman Glitter Hair-n-Nails Playset that Emily *really* wanted and her mother refused to buy. The expression was a mix of hurt and want and fury and . . . before Amanda could name it, Emily whipped her head back around and was gone.

In gym class, Amanda tried again.

But it was track day, and Amanda had to spend extra time in the locker room digging up a supersize sweatshirt to cover her shiny arms, so by the time she made it up to the field, Emily was already sprinting around the track, her long legs striding confidently over the red clay.

The day was exceptionally warm, and Amanda in her bulky fleece was sweating before she even made it around once. She could pour on a little insectile speed if she wanted, but she knew any show of sportiness on her part was bound to make people suspicious. Besides, her scarf was sliding all over the place, so she had to run with one arm up and one down to keep her appendages covered.

She couldn't catch up to Emily. Instead, her former friend lapped her.

"Hey, Emily!" Amanda called as the girl whizzed past. Emily ignored her.

"Emily, listen," Amanda tried again. Useless.

I'll catch her in the locker room, Amanda told herself. Though the mere thought sent chills down her spine. Middle school locker rooms were not for the faint of heart.

Amanda's opportunity came after the bell, when all the other girls had left. Only Amanda, who had to change in a bathroom stall, and Emily, taking care to dust off her pristine white sneakers, remained in the echoey room. Amanda was sure Emily didn't know she was there, because the girl was talking to herself—risky behavior, even for her.

"It's happening to you, too. You're getting powers," she heard Emily say in a mocking voice. "Gross."

Amanda snorted. *Only Emily would think having powers was something to complain about.* She shuffled her feet to make her presence known, and Emily whipped her head around so fast, it was a wonder it didn't snap right off her skinny neck.

"You! Again! Give up!" Emily growled when she saw Amanda peeking around the cage of dodgeballs. She slung her bag over her shoulder and started to leave.

"Wait. Emily, I seriously need to talk to you," Amanda called. "I need you to come over to my house so I can show you some stuff about our moms."

"Oh, come on," Emily spat dismissively. "I told you, my mother is on a cruise. And just because our moms are friends doesn't mean—"

"Do you really think that your mother would leave your birthday party to go on a cruise? Or are you just afraid of what's really going on?" Amanda interrupted.

Emily's bag slid off her shoulder. She turned around to face Amanda with an expression Amanda couldn't quite read—a cross between "I just sucked a lemon" and "you might be on to something"—when Mikki Folders threw open the locker-room door.

"Fiddlesticks!" Amanda muttered.

The instant Little Miss Folders saw Amanda and Emily standing together, her eyes grew wide. The queen of the school fraternizing with a freak was the kind of leverage a gossipy girl—and Mikki was a *very* gossipy girl—could really use. And all three of them knew it. The game had changed.

The only way for Emily to save face now was to appear to be tormenting Amanda—which meant *actually* tormenting Amanda.

Grasping Amanda's arm, Emily started pushing her toward the showers. "Time to clean up, frumpy," she said in a disdainful tone, reaching for Amanda's scarf.

Amanda squeezed her eyes shut. *No! No! No!* The middle school locker room was her personal house of horrors—and the waxworks in this one were coming to life.

"Ziti," Amanda whispered to herself. "Fettuccini, ditalini, tripolini, bucatini!"

"Whoa. What is going on with your arm? It's, like, hard!" Emily gasped and let go. "And why are you talking about carbs?"

Amanda pushed up the sleeve on her jacket. Just enough so Emily could see but Mikki Folders could not. Exposing herself like this was a big risk, but Amanda was out of options.

Emily recoiled. Amanda's arm was hard and shiny, like it was covered in some strange plastic or a thin coating of mother-of-pearl—the flexible, iridescent calcium-carbonate layers mollusks and some cephalopods formed for protection.

Momentarily stunned into silence, Emily looked into Amanda's face and backed away. "Come on, Mikki. I don't have time to clean up this act," she said when she finally found her voice.

Amanda's heart was racing. "Farfalle," she mumbled, naming her favorite butterfly-shaped noodle, and with that, she picked up her pack and raced out of the locker room.

EYE GNAT

Not-So-Fun Bug Fact: Eye gnats feed on human tears and sweat. (Gross!) Male gnat swarms are sometimes called ghosts!

Amanda dashed past the Parsnippity statue and kept on running right off campus. There was still one more period before school was out. She was ditching—something she had never even considered before—and she didn't feel a lick of guilt. In fact, breaking the rules was the only thing making her feel remotely good.

For a moment in the locker room, Amanda thought she was getting through to Emily. There was a look in the other girl's eyes, like a small sliver of light seeping under the door into a pitch-black room. It had given her hope.

Unfortunately the light was extinguished the instant Mikki showed up and Emily's social status was at stake. Her turn was so swift and so mean that it left Amanda breathless and wondering why she thought talking to Emily would help in the first place. How could she have imagined Emily as her ally, let alone her *partner*?

Amanda wiped her moist eyes as she flapped down the sidewalk away from the school in her ridiculously large jacket. The locker-room moment had made her feel exhausted and shaky, but after a few blocks, it began to strengthen her resolve and clarify a couple of things:

1. Never again would she attempt to talk with Emily at school. And while Amanda hoped that her exoskeleton reveal in the locker room had jarred some sense into the younger Battfield, only time would tell.

2. She would not let Emily's attitude stop her. Partner or no partner, she was ready to bust a move!

"Poppy," Amanda called as she stepped into the house. The main room seemed brighter than usual, and Amanda shed her coat and scarf. She was shvitzing like crazy under the hot, scratchy wool. "Poppy?" she called again. Still there was no answer, but it did not take long to find him in the small bungalow. He was in Amanda's mother's bedroom, apparently cleaning out her closets—like *that* was a big priority. He had piles of winter clothes, holiday outfits, and bridesmaid dresses strewn on the bed.

"Your ma developed some strange tastes after I retired, let me tell you what," Poppy said, picking up a pair of acid-wash jeans as if they were a dirty diaper. "Can't say I understand what these are all about." He chucked them into a corner.

Amanda didn't ask why he was going through stored clothing. Yesterday, while she made long lists of pasta shapes, Poppy rearranged all the books on the living-room shelves so the spines were in rainbow order. Her grandfather's actions were strange and his motives were mysterious. But the results could be effective.

fusilli

ravioli

tortiglioni

farfalle

penne

conchiglie

macaroni

ruote

"So, Poppy, thanks for the spaghetti lesson," she said, plopping down on the bed in the piles of clothes. "The mantras came in really handy today, though there were some close calls. I'd love to get some more pro tips from you if you have any, but honestly, I don't think there's time for me to get through your whole list." She looked at her nails and tried to act like shrugging it off was no big deal. "Besides, Emily won't listen to me, like at all, so the partner thing isn't very realistic."

Poppy didn't seem to be listening, either. He didn't even look over at her. He just held up a bold, swirly-print jumper Amanda had never seen her mother wear.

"This has potential," the old man muttered, focusing on the vintage garment as if it were a famous painting. "Yes, indeedy, this one's a keeper!"

Potential for what? Amanda scowled. "Poppy, did you hear me? I need you to listen. I'm ready to rescue Mom."

Poppy backed out of the closet with a pair of platform lace-ups. "Now we're talking," he chortled.

"Well, I'm trying to!" Amanda said, getting frustrated.

Sometimes it felt like she and her grandfather weren't in the same room . . . or even on the same planet! They certainly were not in the same conversation.

"I'm trying to tell you that today was a total waste of time—something we're running out of. Mayor Loafenblatt received a threat yesterday. It said that the whopper of a situation you predicted is coming in a few days! Isn't it time we call the police?" Amanda hadn't talked to the authorities since her first 9-1-1 call after the party. She reached for the phone on the bedside table.

That got Poppy's attention. He smashed down the pile of clothes, put a wrinkled hand on Amanda's, and pushed the phone back onto the table. He looked Amanda in the eyes. "Oh. No." He shook his head. "Can't do that. One step at a time," he cackled. "First of all, you aren't ready. Third, you can't do this on your own—you have to wait for Blondie to come around. I know you think she's ignoring you, but give it time. It won't be long before you've figured out each other's strengths and weaknesses. Then you'll work together like champs. Balance each other out. Best hero team ever, maybe! Yes.

Yes. Yes. You have to wait until the donkey dust settles, then it'll be your time."

"But I've got to do SOMETHING now!" Amanda complained.

"You're right. You've got to do something. How about taking another gander at those folders of your mother's," Poppy said. "You'd best root up some info on who we might be fighting here. It's always better to go into battle knowing what you're up against . . . and I bet there are still some feisty characters out and about who'd like to take Dragonfly down a peg. Your mom fought some doozies in her day."

Amanda's jaw dropped. And not because Poppy was pulling down the box of snow clothes. Researching potential enemies was a straightforward task, and one that actually made sense.

"Now get to it! Skedaddle!" Poppy snapped, waving a pom-pom hat and a pair of padded bib overalls at her.

She hurried to the basement and quickly brought Zephyr to Olympian speed. As soon as the door to Dragonfly's lair opened, Amanda popped off the treadmill and hurried inside. She'd already determined that the files on the desk must be her mother's stack of suspects.

Amanda pulled a chair up to the desk to have another look. She started with the slimmest folder. It was filled with information about Calamity Coven. In her previous review of the file, she'd read that the coven had been a club of crotchety retirees who, angered by what they referred to as "freewheeling youngsters roaming the streets with pegged pants and portable stereos," had decided to take matters into their own hands. They had attempted to wage a war on anyone under the age of forty. Amanda guessed that since each member of the Calamity Coven had been seventy-five or older back in the 1990s, they were no longer a threat. "They'd all be over a hundred by now," she whispered, doing the math in her head and moving to the next folders.

The Porcine Sisters and Dark Tarsier were, according to the clippings, safely locked behind bars, serving time for their dastardly (and weird) crimes. Obsessed with baked goods, the Porcine Sisters had hit all the bakeries in town, stealing cakes, cookies, biscotti, and doughnuts every morning for weeks. Once the bakeries had shut down, the greedy sisters had turned their attacks on home bakers until everyone in Oyster Cove was terrified to so much as butter and flour a pan. Menaced and deprived of pastries, the townspeople were forced to purchase outrageously overpriced brownies and crullers from the Porcine Sisters themselves at bake sales. The twin ladies' ultimate crime had been what they called the Cake Walk of Death! Luckily, Dragonfly and Megawoman had rescued all walk participants, and the Porcine Sisters had been placed in a gluten-free cell and given a long sentence to allow them to ponder their pastry problems.

Dark Tarsier's crimes were too terrifying to even read about. Amanda confirmed he was still incarcerated and closed the cover on that offending monster.

Feeling exhausted and horrified by all that her mom had faced back in the day, Amanda opened the last folder in the stack.

The Exterminator's atrocious crimes gave Amanda the willies. The mere thought of her beautiful invertebrate

MOST WANTED

Dark Tarsier

Crimes: Too terrible to put down on paper. Look them up . . . if you dare.

Calamity Coven

Crimes: Plots to destroy whippersnappers. Crabby harassment of young people.

The Exterminator

Crimes: Plotting to take over the earth. Unorthodox scientific practices. Unethical genetic research.

Porcine Sisters

Crimes: Cake Walk of Death. Pastry theft. Gluttony.

friends being transformed into freakish zombies in order to do the bidding of deranged humans was dismaying to say the least. Shaking off the terror, she continued reading. Her mouth dropped open. She could not believe The Exterminator's horror story had escaped her awareness until now!

After Fritz Von Schlingmann revealed his mutated creatures, he was immediately stripped of his title and

EXTERMINATOR EXTERMINATED FROM SCIENCE LEAGUE

Fritz Von Schlingmann, a once-esteemed geneticist and biologist, has been removed from the science community for his extreme position on arachnid and insect bioengineering. His work has been referred to by some of his peers as a "monstrous disregard and disrespect for nature" and a "misuse of a field that should be used to propel mankind forward, not enslave other species."

The millions of insects and spiders killed in his experiments earned Von Schlingmann the nickname "The Exterminator" while completing his doctorate, but the jury was still out regarding the ethics and social benefits of Von Schlingmann's work, until today.

After presenting to the assembled Science League a body of work that involved the mutation of insects into giant beasts of burden completely obedient to his commands, Von Schlingmann was stripped of his title and removed from his position as Dean of Entomology at Bibelot University.

position, and all his awards and honors had also been taken back. Small clippings revealed that the man effectively lost everything he'd ever owned, including friends, colleagues, and status in the science community. Even his dog, Korv, had been taken from him by an animal-protection group suspicious of his motives around any live critters.

The collective pushed Von Schlingmann to the edge, until at last he did exactly what the Science League had predicted. He used his creations with evil intent.

"Oh my goodness," Amanda breathed. "All those poor bugs." Her eyes darted to the next article, THE EXTERMINATOR'S INFESTATION, where she was aghast to learn that the spurned scientist had unleashed a fleet of his mutated beasts into the Science League's Oyster Cove headquarters during their annual convention. The world's scientific leaders had all been in attendance, and while they were meeting in the main hall, Von Schlingmann had taken over the intercom system and reintroduced himself. The quotation was printed in its entirety:

My fellow scientists, you dared to question my experiments. You feared my creations could be used for evil. Well, now you will experience the truth of your predictions! Now, my esteemed friends, you will cower in fear in the presence of THE EXTERMINATOR!

After delivering his monologue, The Exterminator had ordered his creatures to cover the league's building in a fiber of his own invention—a fiber so strong that manmade tools could not cut it. The scientists had been trapped inside. Held hostage at The Exterminator's mercy. His demands were simple—he wanted control of the

entire world, and if he didn't get it, he would destroy Science League headquarters.

"Typical mad-scientist behavior," Amanda snorted as she continued to read.

Just when it appeared that all hope was lost and that the world would have to bow to The Exterminator's demands, two superheroes had arrived and saved the day! Dragonfly and Megawoman not only captured The Exterminator and foiled his evil plot, but they also used their superstrengths to break through the web surrounding the Science League's headquarters and rescue all the people within. In other words, they kicked butt.

Of course, The Exterminator had vowed revenge against the heroes who had toppled his crazy plan. But no one felt very threatened once he was taken into custody. After a quick trial, the madman was found guilty and thrown into a high-security prison, where he was expected to remain for the rest of his life.

Amanda turned to the computer (Poppy had changed the security protocols so Amanda could use it without causing it to explode) to do a quick check. She went to the

prison-record database and searched Von Schlingmann as she had the other villains. But nothing came up. She expanded her search parameters until she finally found a tiny article that revealed that The Exterminator had "gone missing" from jail a few years after his imprisonment. Law enforcement was reportedly on "high alert," and The Exterminator was listed on the FBI's Most Wanted criminal list. But judging by their actions, or lack thereof, authorities weren't all that concerned. Amanda wondered why.

She tried several more searches, but no one had heard from him since his jailbreak.

Stretching out her stiff neck and arms, Amanda realized that The Exterminator was the only guy on her mother's list whose whereabouts were unknown. A shiver snaked up her spine and her tummy rumbled. Amanda shut down the computer and hurried upstairs to check on her lasagna.

Her mind was still reeling as she set the bubbling casserole on the table. It smelled delicious. Amanda served up two portions, all the while picturing The Exterminator roaming around in some revenge-fueled fury.

"Poppy!" Amanda called out several times. He didn't answer. Finally, she walked to her mother's bedroom to let him know that the food he'd requested was ready. Amanda braced herself for the mess before opening the door, but nothing could have prepared her for what she saw strewn on her mother's bed.

Amanda gasped. "Poppy! How could you?"

15

"I came as quickly as I could," Vincent puffed when Amanda opened the door.

Amanda took a step back to let her friend come inside, and to let him get a good look. She wanted to catch his reaction. She was not disappointed. Vincent clutched the door frame to keep from falling over.

"*Where* did you get that *ensemble*?" he trilled, still panting. Amanda spun around so Vincent could view her outfit from all angles. Her new separates deserved to be admired.

As it turned out, Poppy had more than one trick up his sleeve and had been doing more than sorting out (and holding running commentary on) her mother's old clothes. The "poorly timed" closet cleaning had actually been a fabric raid. Poppy had been mining for makeover fodder, and he'd found it. In spades. An hour alone, a sewing machine, a pair of scissors, and some sticky-back Velcro, and suddenly he had checked another thing off Amanda's list: She had a custom wardrobe fit for an insectile superhero!

With a flourish, Amanda showed off the groovy botanical print on the sheer-sleeve, mandarin-collared tunic Poppy had paired with black leggings. She had to admit she was pretty pleased with the getup. It fit like it had been made for her. Because, well, it had been.

"It's stunning," Vincent said, shaking his head and staring with his mouth wide open like a Papuan frog-mouth waiting for a meal. "And it has pockets?"

Amanda nodded. "There's more, too," she said. But she couldn't talk about what was hiding beneath her outfit—or the other garments and how they made her feel cared for and cute and ready to return to school in spite of the taunts and hazards therein. She was overwhelmed. And a little emotional.

Vincent took a step back and snapped his mouth shut.

"What?" Amanda asked. It was obvious the boy had something to say, and he was afraid she would not want to hear it. "Spill," she demanded.

"The shoes. They're all wrong. You need something shorter. Sharper. Maybe in white."

"Okay, as long as I can run in them."

Vincent stared down at her worn-out boots and then consulted his Casio calculator watch. "We just might have enough time." He nodded.

A few minutes later, Vincent and Amanda were pedaling as fast as they could toward Snifferveldt Square Mall. Amanda felt a little guilty sneaking off and leaving Poppy to do the dishes, but she trusted Vincent's fashion instincts implicitly. The outfit deserved decent footwear, and there wasn't much time. Besides, she had a boatload of information about her mother's potential kidnapper to download to her pal.

"Let's go to the food court!" Vincent shouted over his shoulder.

He was always hungry and he loved people watching.

"Okay. Maybe I'll try that new turmeric-ginger blend they have at the Haight Street Juicery. My mother said it's delicious." Amanda got a lump in her throat at the thought of her mom. It felt more than a little wrong to be at the mall while her mother was being held captive, but she had no choice.

Inside, the shopping mecca was more crammed than usual with people practicing retail therapy to relieve their stress and get new outfits for the Oyster Cove Day celebration. As Vincent navigated the hordes, pulling Amanda along behind him, she had another strange feeling. According to the antennae beneath her stylishly woven headband, somewhere in the retail labyrinth, something was going very wrong.

An alarm sounded, confirming her suspicions, and Amanda froze right outside Cheap and Cheerful.

"Amanda, are you okay?" Vincent asked, staring at her with a look of concern.

"There's something I have to do before we get those shoes," Amanda told her confidant. She grabbed Vincent's arm and pulled him past shoppers and strollers into the maintenance corridor.

The hallway was long, lit by a lone fluorescent tube, and covered in graffiti. The smell of cleaning fluids and just a splash of mildew, or worse, filled the air.

"Gross," Amanda said out loud. But there wasn't time to consider the damage the grime-dissolving chemicals were doing to their brains. She was already changing. Her skin hardened and her feelers pushed against her headband. Amanda did not even bother to ponder pappardelle or orzo. She was doing this.

Vincent stood there, stunned. "Didn't Poppy tell you that you had to keep your . . . stuff . . . under wraps?"

Amanda fixed her friend with a look. "Yes, but somebody out there is doing something bad, and Poppy also said I have to use my instincts and develop my skills. Besides, I really want to give my attire a test run!"

In a series of moves that looked practiced but weren't, Amanda converted her ensemble into a bona fide superhero outfit. She whipped off the tunic to reveal what was basically a set of iridescent long underwear with a short fluttery skirt. With a tug, her black headband turned into a velvety mask shaped like an abstract butterfly. It covered her head, nose, and eyes and was pretty darn cute.

"Epic," Vincent murmured, transfixed by the design. "Your grandfather is a genius."

Amanda nodded in agreement and handed her street clothes to Vincent. She made sure her old boots were laced up tight and double-knotted. Who knew what she was about to get herself into, and tripping over a loose lace would not be very superheroic at all.

"Can you tell it's me?" she asked, straightening up. It was essential that she not be recognized.

Vincent shook his head. "Nope. Not if I didn't know," he said.

Adjusting the mask slightly, Amanda caught a glimpse of herself in the glass panel covering the fire hose. Wearing a superhero costume, a REAL one, made her feel instantly empowered. *Now* she was ready for business.

"Let's see what this outfit's made of." Giving her friend a nod, Amanda dashed out of the corridor and into the middle of the mall. She disregarded the stares of shoppers and workers and zeroed in on the location that had triggered her innate sense of wrongdoing. Within seconds she found herself at the Diamond Factory.

Behind the counter, two sales associates were frantically calling mall security while their manager, a little frazzled fellow, ran around waving his arms in the air as if he were trying to shoo away tsetse flies.

"What's the problem?" Amanda asked, announcing her arrival and demanding an update. (If she was going to be a superhero, she'd have to be assertive!)

The salespeople turned, stunned to find a costumed hero in their midst. "Who are you? It's not Halloween! We've had enough trouble here today!" shrieked the manager, still in a frenzy. Amanda fixed her gaze on the little red-faced man, and he turned and ran into the back room without waiting for a response.

"We were just robbed," one of the salespeople explained. "I've never been so scared in all my life," she added, fighting back tears.

"He took our Dynasty Collection wedding rings! They're our best sellers! We'll go out of business!" the other woman shouted, scared for her future.

"Get the police here. Don't worry—your Dynasty Collection will be fine!" Amanda reassured the women before stomping out of the store and into the mall.

"But wait! Who are you?" the jewelers screamed,

almost in unison. It was too late. Amanda had sprung into action.

A large crowd had gathered in front of the Diamond Factory, drawn by the shrieking, but Amanda didn't pay any attention to them. Her job was justice, and the curious public would just have to watch from afar.

"He went that way!" someone in the crowd screamed.

Amanda was already on it. Her antennae were feeding information into her frontal lobe, leading her through the parting throng toward the source of danger.

Her quarry raced ahead of her, hopping planters and dodging benches. He scrambled around the spewing fountain and headed straight toward the food court. Shoppers around him screamed. A few cheered when they saw Amanda. The criminal glanced back, spotting his pursuer, and began to hurl obstacles into her path.

"As if," Amanda scoffed, righting baby strollers and waste receptacles without losing any time. "There's nowhere to run, scumbag!" she shouted, still gaining.

The thief looked back again. And this time Amanda was close enough to see fear and confusion written on his sweaty face. "Who are you?" he gasped before shoving a huge flavored-ice cart in her direction.

"Wouldn't you like to know?" she shot back, catching the Shorty's Shave Ice stand before it toppled down the escalator. She sent the tropical cart winging back toward the fleeing criminal. Shave ice and syrup spilled out onto the slick tile floor in rainbow hues. The thief fell and slid like an oversize hockey puck right into a table of chafing dishes at the entrance to Lou La Bonte's Country Buffet. There were screams and a huge clash of metal as the carving station went down. The Dynasty Collection thief absorbed most of the impact and a considerable amount of hot au jus.

"That oughta stop this French Dip," Amanda quipped.

But the sopping criminal struggled to his feet and disappeared into the dark interior of the all-you-can-eat restaurant.

"Hey, you might as well give yourself up, mister, because you are totally trapped!" Amanda shouted. She was really getting into this whole being-assertive thing.

Frightened diners waddled out of the food emporium, their gorging interrupted, as Amanda strode in. She jumped up onto a red leatherette booth to get a better view. Food stations were set up all over. There was a cupcake cart, a Belgian-waffle bar, and even a Hoagie Hutte with its own rustic cabin facade.

A crying child scuttled past holding a cone missing its ice cream—a total bummer—but Amanda paid little attention. Focus was key. There would still be time to find a pair of shoes if she could hurry this up.

Checking in with her antennae, Amanda continued her survey of the dimly lit establishment. She could feel that the crook was lurking nearby, but she couldn't pinpoint his exact location.

Then there was a movement behind the Nacho Nosh table, and she heard the crack of a tortilla chip. Amanda launched herself off the leatherette and landed in front of a giant cauldron of orange goo. Her hand shot out, and she tipped the large vat, sending a tidal wave of melted cheddar cascading down the other side of the station.

"Ow! That's hot!" The thief leaped up, fanning himself with his hands to try to stop the burning.

"And cheesy," Amanda added.

The crook looked like the trash can at a carnival, covered in brightly colored syrup, broth, and cheese. Worse than that, beneath the ooze he was wearing jogging pants with sandals . . . and socks. Vincent would have some choice words for this guy when he caught up.

"Okay, crook, you've had your fun. Are you ready to give up and come with me?" Amanda asked, averting her eyes from the tacky footwear.

"What are you, a reject from *The Defenders of Space Sector Six*?" the thief joked, not knowing that he had said something that would cost him dearly.

"No." Amanda wrinkled her nose at the reference to one of the worst live-action superhero shows on TV. Their neon outfits were pure trash, they were completely made up, and their plots were formulaic. "I'm just a girl who has taken a special interest in making sure justice is served," Amanda seethed. "And if I were you, I'd cut the jokes and hand over the jewelry."

The thief didn't take her advice. Instead, the greased-up bandit took off, sliding out of the restaurant and back into the mall.

"Cripes, this guy is not the brightest bulb," Amanda muttered. She followed him out and through the curious crowd, which was growing and blocking her way. Luckily the fluorescent-orange, congealing-drip trail was easy to follow and led her directly to Blast Off! Sugar Emporium—a candy-by-the-pound shop.

The sweet smell wafted out of the retail space and into the mall in a cloud so thick you could practically taste it. Amanda stepped inside the sweet shop, marveling at the enormous clear tubes of every candy imaginable that reached from floor to ceiling like the trunks of trees in a high-calorie forest. There were greasy smudges on many of the confectionery columns, but the place was such a riot of color, Amanda couldn't tell where the creep was hiding. And she was tired of chasing him.

"Last chance, buster," she called. When there was no answer, she gave the closest candy column a mighty shove. It toppled onto the Cinnamon Snippers column next to it . . . which shattered the Fairy Dust and the Cavity Cluster tubes beyond. One by one, the candy containers went over

like dominoes, spilling sweets everywhere and creating a mist of sugar.

The Dynasty Collection thief was the last thing standing. He was coated in brightly colored candy, and it was starting to harden on his cheesy underlayer.

"Ew." Amanda cringed as she neatly pinned the thief's arms behind his back and tied them with a length of curling ribbon from the bag display. "I cannot believe you made me do that. Just look at my costume," she added. There was a small tear in her leggings, and several Creme Volcanoes were stuck to her knee.

"You're coming with me right now," she said, sounding as bossy as possible. "We're going back to the Diamond Factory, you're going to tell them you're sorry, and then you're going to jail."

Locked in her grip, the crook panicked. "What are you doing? Who are you?" he asked again.

"None of your business. I'm just here to let you know that crime doesn't pay," she snapped.

When the shoppers saw Amanda emerge from Blast Off! with the robber in tow, they let out a cheer and

marched with her all the way to the Diamond Factory. The police, who were already interviewing the frazzled manager, looked grateful as well.

"Here you go," she said to the officers.

"Thank you very much for capturing this creep, miss," said one of the officers. "With everything that's been going on these last couple of days, crime has been on the rise. This guy has been on a spree."

"You're welcome," Amanda said, smiling demurely. She suddenly realized that if she didn't get back to Vincent, these characters were going to start asking questions she didn't want to answer—and she would never get her shoes. "Now, if you don't mind, I've got something important to attend to!" she said with a wave.

As she walked away, the bewildered crowd once again applauding, she couldn't help bursting with pride. Fighting crime wasn't so hard. It had turned out not only to be fun but also rewarding. And talking sass to these criminals truly was her pleasure. Her mother had always taught her to speak to adults with respect, but these lawbreakers deserved a tongue-lashing.

Beside the fountain, Amanda found Vincent waiting for her and looking almost as proud as she felt. He was holding a large bag from Pablo's Pumps-n-More Shoe Emporium. "Come on, hero. I think I saw Emily getting a decaf soy caramel frappé matcha-o-latta at the Swirling Bean. We better buzz out of here before she gets a load of you!"

16

A manda's day had been something like a roller-coaster ride, with lots of steep climbs and thrilling loops. Unfortunately, it now seemed to be heading downhill fast. The exhilaration of the mall showdown was over. The adrenaline rush had lasted long enough for her to don her tunic, adjust her headband mask, and get almost home on her bike. But just as she and Vincent started pumping their way up the last hill to Stubby Oaks, the shaking began again. Then came the sirens, flocks of green horror holograms, and something new: a prerecorded announcement from the mayor. The message blared from the Civil Distress System speakers mounted around the city, instructing everyone to go into their homes and "shelter in place" until further notice. Oyster Cove was on lockdown!

"This is ridiculous!" Amanda huffed, dropping her bike on the lawn. "I'm going back down there to show

BUG GIRL SAYS—
BAD NEWS FOR BAD GUYS!

Time's up, tyrant!

No more Miss Nice Girl.

Shut it, turkey!

Cowpoke, you just rode your last ride!

Think again, scofflaw.

Not on my watch!

people that these phantom phlegm globs are nothing for us to be afraid of!" She started to pull her headband down, but she was halted by a rough hand.

"Sorry, Mandy," Poppy clucked. Amanda hadn't even heard him come out. "You heard the mayor. We have to get inside." Then he looked from Amanda to Vincent and back. His eyes lingered on the small tear in Amanda's leggings and then narrowed. "What have you been up to?"

Amanda opened her mouth to explain. Vincent jumped in first.

"Sir, it's my fault. I needed help finding diodes for my Future Scientists Kiosk project. I don't have much time before my big presentation on Oyster Cove Day, so I asked Amanda to go to the mall with me." He flashed a grin at Poppy (who did not appear at all convinced) and then gave Amanda a look that said, *Sorry, I tried*, before turning his bike and pedaling away quickly.

"Diodes indeed," Poppy chuckled, keeping a hand on Amanda's shoulder as they walked up the path to the house. He opened the door and waved her in first. As she passed, he huffed. "You two could have gotten into a whole heap of trouble," he said.

Once they were safe inside, Poppy held out his hand. "Now hand over those superbreeches, young lady. I see they need mending." His expression softened, and he had a twinkle in his eye when he asked, "How'd the rest of it hold up?"

"It was wonderful. It made me feel, well, like a hero. Thank you, Poppy. I had no idea you could do this!" Amanda burbled. "Where did you learn how to come up with such amazing creations?"

Amanda knew that Poppy probably had a whole lecture prepared about rushing out into battle without thinking things through, but he couldn't resist filling her in on more of his story. He waved her over and then patted the cushion next to where he had just sat on the sofa.

"Now, I don't know if you know this about me, but I was a costume designer for big-time Broadway productions in my day. Sewing was my life's work. So when your ma became world-class, I designed her outfit! Yes, every bit of that jazzy Dragonfly number is my handiwork, and don't let anybody tell you otherwise! That copycat Pierre of Bulgaria tried to take credit for it, but your ma set him straight, lickety-split." Poppy fidgeted—thinking about his old couture nemesis seemed to agitate him.

Amanda wanted to hear more. "Was it always so glamorous?" she asked, awed.

"Heavens, no. You should have seen your ma's first costume—before she went pro! Lime-green jogging pants tucked into cowboy boots." Amanda and Poppy laughed at the same time. Poppy held up a hand and struggled to speak. "There's more," he gasped. "She wore swimming goggles to protect her eyes!"

Amanda couldn't picture it. Her mom, for at least as long as she could remember, always dressed simply. Her style tended to be a bit crunchy, but she always kept it tasteful. Goggles? And cowboy boots?

"Once we perfected it, though, Dragonfly's official costume was such a smash hit with the hero community that crime busters everywhere begged to know who had created her outfit. It was battle-ready and totally runway-worthy all at once. It was, if I do say so, divine."

Poppy's pride was obvious, and it made Amanda feel

proud, too. Her grandfather had turned his costuming career from the theater to the world stage. Heroes such as Buckskin Ronald (famous for tackling the Turducken Goblin) and Hyperia Haiku the Weaver of Poem Power had come to Poppy to update their looks—they would accept no one else.

Of course, Poppy reassured Amanda, he only designed for other heroes of the world when he wasn't busy with his first and most important duty—assisting his daring daughter Dragonfly. From his sewing nook in the underground lair, he tracked sinister plots, did background checks on would-be overthrowers of the free world, created a global union of hero helpers, and even designed a gadget or two—whatever it took to help Dragonfly defeat evil.

Amanda listened, openmouthed and staring.

"Ever hear of the Gelatin Wand?" Poppy asked.

"Have I heard of it?" Amanda blurted out. "It's only the weapon that took down Morbiddia le Poeuf and her Ghost Commandos by trapping them in a giant block of cherry-flavored Jell-O!" She was practically clapping.

"That was me," Poppy boasted. "I made that."

It seemed like Poppy could talk about the old days forever, but suddenly he snapped out of his nostalgic reverie. Shaking his head, he sighed and then gave his granddaughter a stern look. Amanda's smile faded as they both remembered that she was in big trouble.

"As fun as all this talk has been, tonight could have ended a lot differently. Use your noodle, Mandy!"

Amanda squirmed as the fun trip down memory lane quickly descended into a guilt trip of epic proportions. She felt trapped like a moth in a jar as Poppy lectured her about the importance of her training. (He had as much to say on that topic as he did about vintage hero fashion.)

"Now, young lady, I warned you about rushing into things. I was worried sick, just like I used to be about your mother before she teamed up with Megawoman." He waved a finger at her. "You need to listen to me. I've had lots of experience with these goings-on."

"But, Poppy, I trusted my instincts, I used my skills, I was superassertive, and my costume was fantastic. Nobody had any idea who I was!" Amanda insisted. She'd felt great and proud. She wanted Poppy to be proud, too.

"But you went without a partner. That's dangerous."

Amanda's assertiveness began to drain. "I had Vincent," she said softly.

"A sidekick is useful, but not a partner." Poppy shook his head. "Don't you worry too much, though. You learned your lesson, and you're home safe." Poppy's cheerful self returned once he'd given his granddaughter an earful. He smiled. "Just don't do it again!"

Amanda tried to return Poppy's smile. But the partner reminder was giving her a pain. She sat quietly as Poppy began to stitch her damaged costume.

Sewing seemed to soothe her grandpa. And it also put him to sleep. Before long, Poppy was snoring loudly, and Amanda was on her way to her room to check on her bug menagerie. That's when things got really weird.

17

he doorbell rang.

In the distance, air-raid sirens still blared, and Amanda wondered who would be ringing the doorbell when they were all supposed to be locked in their homes. She hesitated. Poppy kept snoring. Perhaps Vincent had forgotten something. Only . . . No. This didn't feel like a visit from Vincent. . . . Slowly she walked back down the stairs and opened the door.

There on the porch was the last person Amanda expected to see: Emily. Amanda nearly choked.

Only a few hours ago, Emily had been threatening to demean her in the showers. It was tempting to slam the door in her face, but . . . there had been a change. She did not look as mean. Yes, she still had her trademark lip curl, but she wasn't quite so . . . smug. And she had come to see Amanda.

"Who's your friend?" Poppy was up and suddenly standing behind Amanda.

"This is Emily," Amanda told him. "She's Megawoman's daughter."

Amanda kept her eyes locked on Emily's face, but Emily did not deny it. Something *had* changed.

"Oh, ho!" Poppy cackled. "Little Miss Battfield. Now we're cooking with gas! The two of you will have this solved in no time. No time at all. What we need is ice cream."

Poppy shuffled off to the kitchen before either girl could stop him.

Neither Amanda nor Emily moved.

The silence grew until it was unbearable.

"Come in," Amanda said unenthusiastically. She'd been waiting for this, wanting it, but now that it was happening . . .

Emily stepped inside. She took a breath. "I guess we have to talk," she said finally.

She guesses . . . Amanda bit her tongue to keep from snapping back, "What was your first clue?" *You need her,* she silently reminded herself. *You need her, and she doesn't do anything unless she thinks it's her idea. So just let it be.* It was easier said than done.

Amanda led Emily to the dining-room table. Poppy slapped two towering bowls of ice cream down in front of them, and Amanda dug in. Hindering criminals burned a ton of calories. She was starving! And she hoped that the frozen goodness would make swallowing her pride a little easier.

Emily stirred her ice cream into soup and chatted politely with Poppy, answering his silly questions (What's your favorite tree fruit? Are you allergic to legumes?) while Amanda shot her skeptical looks. The girl's civility was making her nervous.

Then Poppy asked something that snapped Emily out of her pseudo-polite nodding.

"Say, how's that Frida of yours doing? Quite the character, that one." Poppy laughed. "I wouldn't want to be on the wrong side of a fight with her!"

"Wait, what?" Emily sputtered. He had totally caught her off guard.

"Oh, I know a thing or two about the goings-on over at the Battfield house," Poppy added mysteriously. "Frida and me, we go way back."

Emily shuffled in her seat nervously and then made a point of sitting still. Amanda was enjoying watching her squirm—Emily hated to let her emotions show, and this was clearly too much for her.

With one last lick of her spoon, Amanda suggested they go to her room, where, in relative privacy, she suspected Emily would finally say what she had come to say.

Though it was dark in Amanda's bedroom, individual insect cages were lighted—the bulbs provided heat for the more tropical bugs—giving the place a soothing glow. Emily sat down on the rain-forest-themed bedspread while Amanda got busy feeding her pets. She gazed into the tank closest to the bed—it held a praying mantis egg case. Amanda couldn't wait to see the stunning miniature mantises emerge and scurry about. She was planning to release them into her mother's flower bed to eat aphids and other pests and participate in the cottage garden ecosystem. It was going to be beautiful!

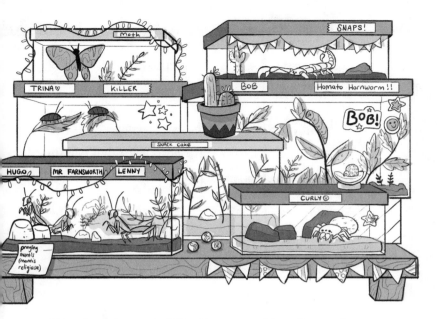

"Earth to Amanda." Emily snapped her fingers impatiently. "Now is not the time to be daydreaming about your little companions. I came here for a reason."

Amanda plopped down on her bed next to Emily. "So . . . ?" She was going to make Emily say it.

"So. I believe you," Emily sighed. "About our moms, I mean."

"Well, you *should*!" Amanda snapped. "I don't lie." She couldn't help but be a little perturbed. Here she was trying to save their mothers, risking everything, and Emily was acting like it was a big deal that she "believed" her.

Emily pursed her lips. Then spoke again. "And . . . I saw you in the mall."

"What do you mean?"

"In your *outfit*," Emily clarified. "With that bad guy? I saw you with your powers, uh, on."

Amanda was shocked. She hadn't thought anyone could recognize her. "Sooooo . . . ?"

"So, if you're going to, like, rescue our moms or something, I want to help."

Emily sounded less self-assured than she had in a long time. But she was saying she was in, that they could be partners, and that meant Amanda was one step closer to getting her mom back. But before they could bust any moves, Amanda had to fill Emily in on a shedload of stuff. Starting with the villain they were up against.

"All right, then. Check this out." Amanda grabbed her mother's folders from her bedside table and plunked them down on her bed beside Emily—she'd been reading them every night. "These are the suspects my mom identified before she and your mom were taken. I've read through everything and narrowed it down. I think this is the guy."

Emily flipped through the clippings. "A bug killer?" she scoffed. "Of course you do."

"A scientist," Amanda corrected. "A really mad one, but I'm not positive it's him. He just seems the most likely."

"So how do we figure out if your bug killer is the one?" Emily asked. "The green things flying all over town don't seem very scientific . . . or buggy." Emily sounded annoyed. Amanda felt annoyed, too. Clearly, she was going to have to do ALL the mental lifting.

"We'll have to go out there and look." Amanda nodded toward her window.

"Now?" Emily asked, arching her perfect brows.

Amanda nodded. "We don't have any time to lose!" She ticked off the steps on her fingers: "We need to track the green monsters back to their point of origin, find the villain responsible for unleashing them, figure out why he needed to keep everyone locked up in fear, foil the plan, and save our moms!"

"Simple," Emily said sarcastically. "You think we can just 'track' those things? If it was that easy, don't you think the police would have done it already?"

Amanda stood up and paced her room. She didn't care for Emily's tone.

"Maybe, but maybe not," Amanda said. "The cop at the mall said there had been a big increase in petty crime. Not to mention a ton of accidents and reports. I think our local law enforcement is pretty tapped out."

"Well, anyway," Emily continued, "I got some stuff from *my* mom's secret lair. Frida took me down there. She knows all about bunkers. And a lot of other stuff, too. It turns out she's been, like, in on our mothers' hero bit for a long time. She's really some famous freedom fighter. And she thinks she owes my mother her life. Apparently after Megawoman and Dragonfly helped liberate her country on spring break, like, twenty years ago, Frida decided to come back with my mother and go into hiding. She thinks it's safer that way. She says if people find out she's really Marvella Corazon, it could jeopardize the safety of her family or something. So she just pretends to clean—and does whatever she can to keep Mom's identity a secret."

Amanda's jaw dropped. *Marvella Corazon? She was a great liberator! She inspired her country to fight an oppressive regime and then disappeared mysteriously . . . into the Battfields' in-law unit?* It was hard to believe.

"Marvella Corazon?" Amanda asked, dumbfounded. "*The* Marvella Corazon?!"

"Or something like that," Emily said dismissively. "Anyway, she told me all that and *then* she showed me Mother's lair. Just wait until you see! It's practically over-flowing with the coolest accessories ever. Including this amazing unitard!" Emily pulled a deep-silver one-piece number out of her bag, her voice rising with excitement. "I mean, can't you just picture me in this?"

Sure she could, but . . . "Emily, this is weird," Amanda interrupted, holding up a hand. Everything was happening so quickly.

"What's weird?" Emily asked.

"You. You . . . walking in here and acting like every-thing's okay. With us. You could apologize, you know. You could do *something*. Do you have any idea what it's like to have your best friend from birth just turn on you and sud-denly act like you're the biggest, grossest joke ever played on the planet? It's not something you forget." Amanda had never spoken to Emily about what had happened between them before. It was hard to say the words, but . . . Amanda blinked back tears. She was strong. She could do this. She was assertive now. Right?

Emily was silent for a moment. She gulped, and Amanda thought her eyes were glistening, too. Just a tiny bit. "Amanda, forget that stuff. This is not about you. Or me. It's not about us. It's about our moms now. We've got to save them." Emily's demeanor changed again, back to sassy. "Whining and moaning are not going to help," she said, and turned away.

Just like that, the tone Amanda had become accustomed to hearing from Emily was back, and there had been no apology. But at least now Amanda's eyes were dry. Quite frankly, Emily's brattiness helped. It was easier to feel angry with Emily than it was to feel sad about their lost friendship. Emily was probably right. It would be best to keep emotions at bay. The two of them didn't have to be friends. They had to be partners.

And they had to get moving.

Without wasting another moment, Amanda snuck

downstairs to retrieve her outfit from the mending basket while Emily changed. Luckily, Poppy was dozing again. Though she had pretty much completed everything on his superhero list, she worried he might insist that Emily do more training, too, or enlist the two of them to help alphabetize the spice drawer, or . . . It would be easiest to just sneak out.

Amanda's garment was lying beside Poppy, perfectly stitched. She paused and kissed her grandpa's hairless forehead. Even though he could be hard to understand, she was glad he was there.

When Amanda returned, clad in her own costume, Emily was admiring herself in the reflection of the mantis tank. "I look amazing, don't I!" Emily exclaimed. It wasn't a question, but Amanda had to admit Emily *did* look great. Like a superchic speed skater—but she wasn't about to tell her that. Instead, Amanda pulled on her mask and let nervous anticipation of what was coming next extend her antennae. With her sensilla in action, she could feel that Poppy was in REM sleep . . . and starting to stir.

"Let's go." Emily turned and stared. She hadn't seen

Amanda's antennae close up before. She started to reach for them, and Amanda pulled back. "Don't touch," she said. "They're sensitive." Then she pushed up her sleeve to show off her crystalline carapace once more. She rapped it with her knuckle. Emily was speechless. Amanda smiled. Even clad in her enviable, shiny, high-dollar Lycra number, Emily had *nothing* on her.

The girls tiptoed past Poppy, pulled the front door shut, and strode out into the crisp night air.

The green monsters were swirling around Stubby Oaks, flying up to people's windows and screeching into their homes menacingly. After Emily flinched a few times, Amanda convinced her that the beasts were nothing to be afraid of. She even got Emily to run through a few of the floaters as they zoomed toward her.

"This is easy," Emily boasted after charging through a chameleon-headed wildebeest with her eyes screwed shut. "We'll take care of this mess in no time!"

Amanda hoped she was right.

The pair walked right through the middle of town, past OCMS, past the heaps of damaged cars and fallen

lampposts—trying to trace the holograms back to a central location. They seemed to be coming from the East Side.

After walking for what felt like hours, Amanda spotted something promising far in the distance. It looked like little green sparks lifting off a malevolent campfire.

"Look! There! They're coming from over there!" she yelled, grabbing Emily's wrist and dragging her toward the launching point.

When the two girls reached their destination on the edge of town, they stopped and stared. Just yards away, the apparitions were rising up, one by one, expelled from the earth by the same evil that was holding their mothers prisoner. They'd found the source!

Emily let out a horrifying wail. "Not that," she moaned. "Oh, anything but that."

They were standing at the entrance to the city dump.

18

"**O**h no, no, no, no, no, gross. Gross. No. Ew," Emily shouted, pacing back and forth. "NO. I can't do it. I won't!"

The two girls had paused at the entrance to the municipal landfill. The rank and fetid spot before them was piled high with disgusting debris from all over the area. It was foul, indeed. Driving past the waste dump on the freeway was an event that called for rolled-up windows, plugged noses, and shrieks of horror. The odor was so strong that the landfill had received the nickname Armpit Acres.

As Amanda and Emily peered at the revolting heap—filled not only with the slimy refuse of today but also with rusting cars, tires, motor homes, and other former treasures now deemed too toxic for landfills—they reconfirmed what they had seen. This was the place the menacing monsters were coming from. They stared in awe and horror as a fluorescent-green pig-goat with bat wings slithered out from behind a half-buried car's shattered windshield and fluttered off menacingly.

Amanda grabbed Emily's arm, relieved to have a partner to brave the ick with—even if it was one with a bad attitude—and started down the hill to investigate.

"Wait. Stop. I'm not ready for this," Emily whined, digging her heels into the dirt. "I can't."

Amanda stopped. "What?" She couldn't believe that Emily could have come so far only to be immobilized by the idea of getting dirty.

"Are you serious right now? It's just trash. Our moms might be down there!" Amanda hissed, pointing to the refuse in front of them. "None of this will hurt you!"

She stood, waiting for Emily to relent, but it was obvious that Emily was not going to budge. In fact, she looked as if she might explode from terror as she stared at that dump.

"Fine. You stay here. Me? I'm going in there to figure out who's behind this and get our moms." With a huff of disgust, Amanda took off. She marched past the barbed-wire arch and stacked tires that created a makeshift entrance to the refuse refuge and headed toward the green glow.

She zeroed in on the toxic spot, waiting for fear to enter her bloodstream, but the fear never came. She was filled with nothing but fierce determination. Within moments, Amanda was close enough to conclude that the broken windshield she had seen from afar was, in fact, part of a mostly intact car—but more important, it was also the entryway of a much more sinister-looking tunnel.

As stealthily as possible, Amanda climbed onto the hood of the rusted automobile and peered past the glass into the portal of doom the glow bubbles had come from. The tunnel was very deep. And the faster she got in there, the sooner she would get away from the overpowering stench of rancid food, ripe diapers, and general decay that was burning into her nostrils.

"Why did it have to be Armpit Acres?" she mumbled, glad she hadn't exhibited outward feelings of disgust while she had been with Emily. One whiner was enough in this hero duo. Too many, really. She took a deep mouth breath and braced for her descent.

As she scurried into the dark passageway, a blast of dry, cold air greeted her. Amanda's skin glowed very faintly and helped guide her way, as did the sensations her antennae were picking up and relaying to her brain. Without her fab feelers, she would have been bouncing off walls.

A dim light ahead grew stronger, and Amanda moved toward it until finally the tunnel opened onto a dank corridor with high, ominously angled ceilings. A bubble beast came hurtling toward her, grimacing, but she paid the translucent jerk no mind.

"Emily's missing out on all the action," Amanda said to herself as she emerged from the nasty tube. Letting her instincts guide her, she walked toward a sound coming from the next cavern—a mechanical hum. Her antennae twitched. She could feel electrical impulses before she saw the massive computer bank. The haphazard network looked like it hailed from the dawn of time; each machine's case was that ugly off-white that yellows with age into the color of rancid butter. Black screens blipped with bright green letters and symbols. These computers were way past their prime, connected to one another by a sketchy patchwork of cables and wires that looked like the ultimate fire hazard.

The room opened farther, revealing a massive, dimly lit space. Towering overhead was an enormous mega-computer that Amanda had to assume was some sort of command center. Giant lights flashed and blinked, and ancient-looking knobs stood ready to activate the contraption and enable it to perform tasks that a pocket calculator could probably accomplish in half the time. The monstrosity was hooked up to yet another machine in the next room that also looked as if it belonged in a museum, not in a currently operating Den of Evil.

Amanda followed the connections until a soft, squelching noise and a strong wind made her pause and cover her eyes. When she uncovered them, she saw a different appliance blowing great, green, slimy bubbles that transformed with a *POP!* into the vaporous ghouls that were terrorizing Oyster Cove.

POP! A scorpion-tailed bison emerged and soared out of the tunnel toward town.

POP! A snake with a hyena mane and sharp teeth slithered through the air and away.

Every cell inside Amanda was on high alert. Her antennae were sending danger signals so strong that Amanda felt rather zingy. She knew the green things were harmless, but she was sure their creator was lurking nearby. She found herself wishing Emily hadn't backed out. Indeed, a partner would be a good thing to have right about now.

She jumped when she heard the raspy voice.

"What's this?" the voice demanded.

Behind the emerging monsters, a puny man sat huddled over the keyboard of his computer. He moved stiffly, taking his eyes from the screen and blinking like a person just waking up.

"What's this?" he rasped again, attempting to swivel in his ancient chair. His feet dragged limply against the stone floor,

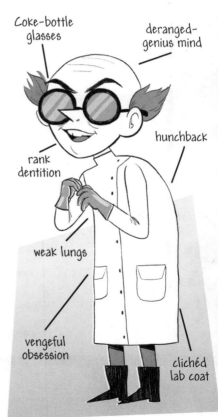

Coke-bottle glasses

deranged-genius mind

hunchback

rank dentition

weak lungs

vengeful obsession

clichéd lab coat

hardly making a shuffle. This guy, much like his contraptions, was old and barely functional.

Amanda had no answer to his question. The leering green monsters beginning to encircle her were not doing much for her clarity of thought, either—solid or not.

"Who are you?" the man demanded, more irritably.

"Who are *you*?" she shot back, though she was pretty sure she knew. "And what do you think you are doing with these . . . bubble beasts?" Insulted, the beasts pressed closer.

The man stood up. He was shorter than Amanda, or maybe he just couldn't straighten his spine. He was wearing a long dingy lab coat, and Amanda half expected to see dust rise off him when he moved. The hint of a smile tugged at one corner of his mouth, making it open slightly into a leering snarl. Yes, she had definitely seen this guy before.

"You like my pets?" the nasty man croaked, displaying more of his yuckmouth.

Amanda cringed at the sight of his teeth. From behind purple lips, a row of yellowed and blackened nubs revealed themselves, resembling a particularly nasty blue cheese. She shivered in disgust.

"Call them off," she commanded. "Your . . . whatever-they-ares have wrecked Oyster Cove and are scaring law-abiding citizens. You've got to stop this. Now!"

"Did you hear that?" the little man said, mumbling in the general direction of his shoulder. "She wants me to call you all off." He punctuated his last word with a wave of his hand, and the beasts hovered ever closer.

The underground lair smelled sulfuric and was making Amanda feel clammy and claustrophobic, like she'd had way too much egg salad and Easter candy.

"Could you back off, please?" she asked, irritated. When nothing moved, Amanda cried out, "Get these things away from me right now! Or else I'll . . . I'll . . ." She wasn't sure what.

It was clear these beasts were not going to back down, and Amanda was fed up. She'd had it with these creeps! With a focused burst of energy, she did a remarkable spin-turn and kicked one of the more prickly specimens. Her boot sailed through the green fog unscathed, and the apparition, disappointed that its secret had been revealed, floated off to sulk in a corner.

"That's right, pinhead," Amanda said, cocking an eyebrow. "I know all about your flock of fake fiends."

The aged nerd took two steps backward, stunned by Amanda's brashness. The look on his face said it all. Amanda was the first person to challenge his creatures. Ever. She was supposed to have run away crying. . . .

"So, who'd you say you were?" Amanda asked.

"*I* am The Exterminator," the deranged old man answered pompously. He turned around to press a few keys on his computer, and seconds later the hologram monsters vanished. "And *you* have a surprising amount of backbone . . . for a little girl."

"Exoskeleton," Amanda corrected him. Some scientist this guy was. It was obvious that the fabulous armor encasing her was not coming from her spinal region or anywhere else *inside* her.

The Exterminator sniffed. "Hmph. Well, then, I've told you who I am. Now tell me who you are. And how did you get here?"

Amanda had come for answers, and now this crabby geezer was asking all the questions. She thought it best not to reveal, just yet, that her mother was this guy's sworn enemy and that she was there on a rescue mission.

"Come on, then. Out with it. I asked who you are, and what you are doing here, and I want to know now!" the so-called scientist said testily.

"I'm . . . Bug Girl," Amanda answered finally. Why she offered up the name her hateful classmates used to taunt her to this withered bully, Amanda would never know. But it felt right—and good—to *own* it.

"I am Bug Girl," she repeated. "I'm here to stop you!"

The Exterminator attempted to laugh out loud but got too winded. He clutched the back of his chair and wheezed his amusement instead.

Amanda scowled. Insensitive chortling rankled her. She glared at the doctor's hairless, wrinkled pate as he leaned down to type something into his keyboard. He hunched farther, trying to keep her from seeing what was on his screen.

"Bug Girl," he muttered, shaking his head.

"That's right," Amanda snapped back, growing more irate. "And you need to listen up. Your monsters are destroying the town and ruining everyone's evenings, and we are not going to stand for it!"

"Child," the aged villain said dismissively, "you're obviously aware of how 'harmful' my monsters are. The *people themselves* are destroying the town. Panicking, screaming, driving into things. Humans never stop to think. I'm just shocked that you—barely out of training pants—got up the courage to drag yourself here and face them."

Training pants? Oh, that was it. Amanda was not going to let this doddering old creep mock her. Bug Girl was not going to be mocked anymore. She'd had enough.

Moving quickly, Amanda reached out and grasped the top of The Exterminator's wheeled desk chair. With one arm, she sent the chair flying to the other side of the room with the mad scientist still sitting in it. With her other hand, she picked up the computer keyboard and brought it crashing down on the monitor.

"Where on earth did you come from?" The Exterminator gasped as he rolled to a stop. He was not expecting such force from a sassy girl in an insect costume. "Surely you're not from that putrid town. In case you hadn't figured it out, I hate Oyster Cove. I hate it!"

"You guessed it, genius," Amanda snapped. "I am Oyster Cove born, and proud of it."

Amanda's town pride triggered something in The Exterminator. His expression changed from perplexed fear to smug certainty. He teetered toward her with an accusing finger extended, thrusting it back and forth.

"Oh! *You!* I know who you are! I should have known

the moment you buzzed in here with your sad, shiny, pathetic little exoskeleton. *YOU ARE JUST LIKE YOUR MOTHER!*"

"Yes I am, turkey, and you're about to get roasted!" Amanda snapped back.

"I should have known that goody-two-shoes nit-wit would have a child," he seethed, rubbing his hands together in anger. "ONE of her walking around on the planet was bad enough. But then she had to go and make another goody-goody who's just as obnoxiously anxious to make sure justice is served, the innocent are protected, and all of that simpleminded folderol."

The Exterminator spoke about Dragonfly with such venom that he was practically foaming at the mouth. His hateful babble confirmed beyond any doubt Bug Girl might have had that this was the guy who had kidnapped her mom!

"Where is she?" Amanda yelled, positioning herself for battle. "Hand her over!"

"I couldn't possibly let that menace roam around free any longer, could I? She and her perky, perfect partner—

they took everything from me. My hopes and dreams were dashed by uppity girls in tiresome costumes. But I'll make them pay. You'll see. I'll make you ALL pay. This year, Oyster Cove Day will be a celebration like this town has never seen before!"

So the old cretin was keeping everyone cowering so he could serve up his brand of bitter justice on Oyster Cove Day, when an audience was assured.

"Your experiments on insects and arachnids were unethical and downright disgusting!" Amanda screeched.

"Ah, touched a feeler, have I?" The Exterminator asked as he hobbled over to a separate computer station that had not been damaged during Amanda's power tantrum. Lowering himself into a seat, he sounded overjoyed.

"I have your mother, all right." He cackled pompously. "I've been keeping her under wraps, so to speak, while I put the finishing touches on my ultimate revenge plan for her, her revolting partner, and this nasty little town of yours."

Amanda fidgeted. There was something that didn't jibe

with her research. "If you're The Exterminator, what's with the green monsters? Why aren't you using your armies?"

"Ah, you're a clever one, aren't you? And you've done your homework. The hologram monsters are merely a distraction, child. I wanted to draw your mothers out without letting them know exactly whom they were dealing with. If I had unleashed my *fabulous* mutated insects at the start, those two dullards would have gone into battle prepared, and where's the fun in that? I surprised them with my genius, and they were overwhelmed by my trap."

Amanda groaned aloud. This pinhead was a little too boastful.

"With Mommy and Company out of commission," he continued, "I felt certain there were no other obstacles in my path to vengeance. But then"—he swiveled back around to face Amanda and scowled—"you arrived."

Amanda gulped. Even though the aged archvillain seated before her looked more like a zombie shuffleboarder than a threatening mad scientist, too much was at stake here for her to mess this up.

"Listen, loser, do you mind if I just blow up this burrow so we can get on with our lives?" she snapped. The Exterminator swiveled around so his back was to her and made a dismissive motion with his hand. "It's either that or you can tell me where my mother is, and I can drag you off to the police without further violence."

To her surprise, The Exterminator continued to ignore her. He didn't even seem to hear her. He just sat there, pecking at his gigantic keyboard and saying, "Oh, good, very good," over and over again.

"Excuse me," Amanda prodded. "We were kind of in the middle of something here?"

"And now," The Exterminator replied snippily, "we no longer are. You may leave, child. You'll get nothing from me."

Amanda didn't like The Exterminator's attitude. Bug Girl would not be dismissed.

In an instant, she sprang into the air and landed directly in front of the bank of rickety computers. Without conscious knowledge of what she was doing, she released a repetitious percussive noise that increased in frequency until its decibels blew out the computer system. Smoke

poured from the old reel-to-reel tape decks that backed up The Exterminator's information. Monitor glass shattered. Sparks flew from all the hardware in the room. Then everything went black.

"Tymbals," Amanda murmured in the darkness. "I've got tymbals!" She was overwhelmed and delighted to share the same sound-producing organs that cicadas used to create their summertime hum. And hers were supercharged. It seemed her awesome new tymbals had wiped out the entire computer bank!

But then one computer hissed and sparked back to life, offering a low glow.

"Dang," Amanda mumbled to herself. She squinted through the smoke toward the spot where The Exterminator had been sitting. He was not there.

A scuffling sound behind her made her whirl. In the clearing haze, she made out a number of dark tunnel entrances she hadn't noticed before. They branched out of the room in eight directions—The Exterminator could have fled down any one of them!

CICADA

Fun Bug Fact: Cicadas have tymbals—sound-producing organs that consist of alternating stiff and flexible membranes and a large sound-amplifying chamber. The cicada's loud call is produced by using muscles to rapidly move the membranes, which makes a loud clicking sound.

20

Before Amanda could jet into action and find the sinister creep, the reactivated computer in front of her started blinking frantically. She heard a finger tapping against a microphone and then a cackle echoed in the cavernous room. "In case you're still rooting around in my laboratory, Larva Lass, or whatever your vulgar little name is," a seething voice chuckled over a loudspeaker, "you might want to evacuate. Now that Phase One has been completed, we can't have you snooping around."

Smug jerk, Amanda thought. But before she could say anything smart, the voice continued.

"Oh, how I've suffered at the hands of your mother and her associate. You have no idea what I've been through since I escaped that dreadful prison—living in the lowest little rooms, hovering over the notes and books I managed to spirit away before they raided my offices," The

Exterminator wheezed into his microphone. "I've had to cobble everything back together from memory and scraps. Years, it's taken. Long, horrible years in seclusion, working tirelessly for revenge. And I shall have it!"

Amanda was floored. As she scrambled to figure a way out, The Exterminator kept talking. Apparently all that alone time had made him desperate for an audience, even if it was the daughter of one of his archenemies.

"This underground pit is, as I speak, filling up with methane," he said. "The authorities won't notice the poison, given all the toxic gases lingering in this landfill. That is, if they even bother to come looking for you. In approximately two minutes," the loudspeaker wheezed, "the air will be too noxious for you to survive in. That should give you just enough time to give your antennae a real workout." He gurgled oddly. Perhaps it was a laugh.

"Where's my mother?" Amanda screamed.

"Oh, not to worry. Mommy is fine. I wouldn't dream of hurting her until my plan is complete, child."

The Exterminator's pompous tone was annoying.

"You see, the time has come for Phase Two, the part

where I exact my revenge. Oh, it's all devilishly clever. . . . Too bad you won't be around to see it."

The direness of the situation didn't keep Amanda from groaning.

"What do I have to do to get my mother back? Do you have, like, demands that need to be met, or are you just going to push people around so you can feel better about yourself?"

"No. No demands, my puny little pupa," The Exterminator snipped back. "Just justice."

"Justice? I'm *so* sure," Amanda spurted. "You don't even know what that means."

"Regardless, Maggot Miss, I plan to take over the world using my delightful army. And there's not a single thing you can do about it. Oyster Cove's so-called heroes are out of the picture, and the gas you're breathing is already ravaging your system. Your little act of defiance actually did me quite the favor. When my plan comes to fruition, it shall do so unhindered."

"We'll see about that," Amanda said, attempting to sound stronger than she felt.

"Enough of this useless prattle!" the villain finally snapped. "Only one of these tunnels leads to the surface, and it's lights-out for you, Bug Girl."

The loudspeaker blasting The Exterminator's voice shut off with a thunk. The last flickering computer blinked out, and Amanda was left in total darkness.

"Crap," she blurted, not really sure how she could possibly get out of this. No light penetrated the lab at all. She groped in the gloom for any of the eight tunnel exits. She tripped over wires and computer components.

And then she remembered—earlier, when she was all fired up and heading into this pit, her abdomen had emitted a faint bioluminescent glow. She might have the capability to light up like a firefly—but for some reason her lumens didn't seem to be turned on anymore. How could she trigger the process needed to light up the night and get out of this dump before it imploded?

Amanda racked her brain. She recalled that some lampyrids emitted a constant glow for a few hours a day, and that clearly wasn't the case with her. She seemed to have traits similar to those of good old North American fireflies. They glowed in two situations: one, to attract a mate, and two, to ward off predators. That first situation was clearly out of the question—*ew*—but she could definitely use a warning light to keep creeps away. She focused her mind, willing herself to *feel* predators all around her. *I am a firefly*, she told herself, *pulsing in the night!*

She began to breathe deeply. Oxygen was necessary for the chemical reaction that gave fireflies their signature feature, and she hoped there was enough of it left in the methane-laced air. She felt a tingle and thought she saw a faint hint of light. She breathed faster, filling her lungs, and the light pulsated like a fire being fanned. It was working! But she had to move to get out before the methane sapped her. She also had to be careful not to hyperventilate—passing out could be her final mistake.

Rushing toward the tunnel entries, she wished she could remember which one she'd used to get into this mess. She couldn't smell the gas mixing with the stale oxygen of The Exterminator's lair. But she could feel it. She started to get a bit woozy.

She peered into each of the tunnels, hoping for a sign

to lead her out of this nightmare. And then she smelled it. The rotting stink of Armpit Acres. It permeated her olfactory senses. It made her eyes water and her nose wrinkle. But at the same time, she had never been so happy to be assaulted by the putrid odors of decaying garbage. Her senses would lead the way out of this mess!

Her antennae squirmed and led her toward the tunnel that was the most fragrant with filth. Up she scrambled through the darkness until she was pulling herself around the broken windshield she'd ducked under and was outside and away from The Exterminator's chamber of evil.

In the distance, Emily jumped up and down and waved, screaming Amanda's name frantically.

But Amanda heard nothing. As she stood up, she felt the full impact of the gas she'd been exposed to in the pit. She blinked her eyes a few times. Her vision blurred. She tried to call out but instead collapsed onto the car hood, unconscious.

FIREFLY

Fun Bug Fact: The firefly is a beetle, not a fly. It has special cells that create a chemical called luciferin and an enzyme called luciferase. Luciferin combines with oxygen in the air to make a molecule called oxyluciferin, and that reaction is sped up by the luciferase—to create LIGHT!

21

A warm light greeted Amanda when she next opened her eyes. Her vision remained fuzzy, but she could make out one of her beloved spiders in a tank beside her. She realized she was in her own bedroom, tucked under layers of blankets. She was still wearing her costume and headband. A humidifier hummed nearby, pumping out thick clouds of eucalyptus-infused steam.

Amanda strained her eyes to see more. The figure slumped over in the chair by her bed had to be Poppy. He stirred as he realized she was awake. "Back with us, are you?" he asked gently.

"Poppy, what happened? I remember being in the dump, and now . . ." Amanda sputtered. Her voice was raspy and her vision refused to clear. She was confused but alive.

"Your little friend called me. The prim one. Said youwere at the landfill. I thought it was a bunch of poppycock, but then she said I'd better hurry because it didn't look good. She was right. . . . When I got there, you were out cold. But you're up and at 'em now, thank goodness!" Poppy smiled weakly.

Amanda swallowed. Her throat was sore. Her head pounded. So Emily hadn't completely deserted her, after all. She wondered briefly if she might even owe her life to Emily. But she didn't want to think about that too hard. She still felt horrible; she was barely able to move, and her lungs ached. Wait. Everything ached. And her mouth was desert dry.

"Where's Emily now?" she asked, puzzled.

"Oh, that delicate little flower called for Frida to come fetch her once I got there and she knew you were safe." Poppy chuckled. "Kept flapping her gums about needing a shower and something called an 'exfoliant,' whatever sort of newfangled tomfoolery that is. Frida gave her an earful, too. You would have been proud. Called her 'the little princess.'"

Amanda attempted to sigh. Even in the direst of situations, Emily remained totally prissy.

"Poppy, could I have some water?" she asked.

"Sure thing, Mandy," he said, shuffling to the door.

With Poppy gone, Amanda thought she was alone but then heard sniffling. She turned her head with great effort and saw Vincent in a nearby beanbag chair, puffy-eyed and wilted. Tears were streaming down his face.

"Vincent?" Amanda whispered. "What are you doing here?"

"I heard a car pulling into your driveway." Vincent sniffled, trying to pull himself together. "When I looked out my window, I saw your grandfather carrying you in. I ran over as fast as I could, and he said I could stay, but only for a minute."

Amanda was thankful to have a friend at her side. She thought maybe Poppy was wrong about a partner being more important than a sidekick. Sidekicks were loyal.

"Vincent, listen to me," she huffed. She had a lot to tell him and not much time. It was getting harder to breathe. "You know more about what's going on here than anyone else, and I need you to talk to Emily and help her out if anything happens to me."

"What do you mean? What could happen?" Vincent slobbered, wiping away fresh tears. "You're here and awake! You're going to get better! And why would I ever help that stuck-up social climber?"

Amanda struggled to sit up. "The Exterminator poisoned me when I was in his lair," she explained. "I don't know what's going to happen, but you need to be prepared. You can do this! Now pay attention."

Vincent scooted his beanbag closer to Amanda's bed. She flopped back against the pillows. She felt like she was about to pass out at any second and was having trouble keeping her eyes open.

"Emily's not as mean as she seems to be." Amanda struggled to keep speaking. "I think, especially after today, that she's just scared. Scared to be herself, maybe."

Vincent was taken aback. He looked like he'd seen someone dressed in florals *and* plaids. Amanda was defending Emily, the girl responsible for all her misery!

"Emily and I, we take after our moms," Amanda continued. "We've both got powers. And I think I know what hers is, even if she hasn't figured it out yet. Emily's got . . . an anger-management thing happening. You've got to get her upset to help her unleash superstuff. And we're going to need that stuff unleashed if we want to defeat The Exterminator and save the town on Oyster Cove Day."

Vincent was speechless. Amanda knew it was a lot to take in. She was telling him he would have to work with Emily, the unapproachable. Emily, the Queen of Mean. Emily, who had never learned his name and, when forced to acknowledge him, usually called him Marmoset. This was the person Amanda insisted Vincent work with in order to salvage Oyster Cove's freedom. She was asking a lot. But no more than she knew he could handle.

"Wh-what do I need to do?" Vincent managed to squeeze out through gulps of air and bouts of panic. He didn't like confrontation to begin with, and Emily Battfield was not a person to be confronted.

"You need to make fun of her," Amanda said in a whisper. "You need to make fun of her in public, and about her appearance. Especially her clothes. If her hair looks greasy, tell her. If her shoes are scuffed, make sure to point it out. You have to be awful! Use words like *cheap* and *knockoff* and *frumpy*. Maybe even *last season*. The angrier you get her, the closer she'll get to tapping into her powers. She's almost there. I've seen her snap things in half." Amanda paused. Partially for effect, but more to catch her breath. She was fading fast.

"But be careful," she warned her friend. "Emily doesn't know how strong she is. Once you start in on her, you might have to take cover. She might not have much control. Anything could happen."

Vincent was smiling now, despite the situation.

"What?" Amanda asked.

"I'm sorry, but this assignment is going to be totally fun," Vincent said. "Did you know that I've been waiting for months to tell her that black shoes should never be worn with a brown belt?"

Amanda breathed out a pathetic puff of air that should have been a laugh. Her eyes were closed now, and breathing was increasingly difficult. Her pale skin had taken on a pallid, pasty off-white hue.

"Amanda?" Vincent touched her arm and recoiled. A

fine white film had settled over her body—a sort of fuzz. Barely visible, it coated everything. Even her eyelids.

"Vincent"—Amanda turned—"feed my bugs. Instructions are on my desk. And, Vincent," she whispered, "I know you can do this. Thank you for being my friend."

Determined to stay awake, Amanda saw Poppy returning with a pitcher of water and some cookies on a tray. Next to her, Vincent sat with his face buried in his hands.

Poppy put the snack down and shuffled over to Amanda's bedside. He put his hand on the whimpering boy's shoulder.

"Now, don't you worry too much." Poppy patted Vincent. "These things—they tend to have a way of working themselves out. You'll see. Run along home now."

Vincent looked back once and waved as he left the room.

Amanda struggled to say something, and then everything went black.

Vincent's Fashion Dos and Don'ts!

<u>Do</u>

- Wear clothes that fit (tailoring is everything).
- Own it!
- Take risks.
- Go retro!
- Try it in black! Goth can be fun.
- Stay true to yourself.

<u>Don't</u>

- Wear black shoes with a brown belt.
- Supersize it.
- Get your panties in a bunch— too small is too bad.
- Mix plaids and florals.
- Tuck in your sweaters.
- Overaccessorize.

Emily remembered the *first* time she tried to make the break with Amanda like it was yesterday. It wasn't a mean thing; at least, that's not the way she saw it. It was just . . . necessary. It started when Amanda called her up to coordinate outfits for a presentation on Abel Goatslam and the Curd Boom of 1812 that the two of them were doing in front of the school for Heritage Days. Amanda thought it would be "cute" if they wore the matching Clam-I-Am T-shirts they purchased together at the pier over the summer. "It'll be fun. Like we're twins!" Amanda suggested gleefully. Emily knew for a flat-out fact that there was nothing fun about the idea. They were already giving a speech about curdled dairy. That, coupled with wearing matching seafood outfits in front of the whole school, would result in nicknames and worse.

Still, Emily hadn't wanted to be the one to break

it to her clueless friend. Amanda's wide eyes, her trust, her heart-on-her-sleeve personality . . . She probably should have told Amanda, "No way. That is a terrible idea." But she couldn't. Instead she let Amanda show up in her goofy T-shirt while she chose to wear a cute blouse. There would be no "twinsies" on her watch.

The hurt look on Amanda's face when she saw Emily and realized she hadn't put on her coordinating tee was hard to take. Harder to take, Emily knew, would have been the mocking judgments of the other fifth-grade girls.

"Sorry," she told Amanda. Though Emily was not sorry about dodging the social bullet. She reminded herself that she had done her friend a favor. She had done them *both* a favor. If they'd made such a dire fashion slip in tandem, they would *both* have become a laughingstock and slid so far down the social ladder that they never could have climbed back up. It was then that Emily realized she would have to let Amanda go to save her. And herself. See? She had *saved* Amanda . . . that time.

But what about now?

Emily was racked with guilt. She felt like everyone she

met was staring at her and knew what a wimp she'd been in the face of danger.

It might be different if she had powers. The thought of *that* horrible injustice made Emily's cheeks grow hot. It wasn't fair that Amanda had cute little superantennae and who-knew-what-all else! The glimpse she got in the locker room of Amanda's glossy body armor had set Emily off completely. Until then she'd almost convinced herself that her mom really *was* on a cruise and that Amanda was plain nuts. But then . . . proof.

Emily was nearly hysterical by the time Frida arrived to pick her up early from school after that incident.

They rode home in silence, but once they were inside, Frida took Emily by the hand and led her all the way to the back of her mother's largest walk-in closet.

"It's time you knew, *mija*," Frida said in a grave tone. "Past time, if you ask me." Then Frida pushed a button on the mirrored wall behind Emily's mother's prized collection of organic yoga pants, and the floor began to move. Together Emily and Frida descended into an underground area as big as the house above it.

"Listen to me carefully," Frida said. She kept looking deep into Emily's eyes without smiling. It made Emily feel all squirmy and weird. "I owe your mother my life," Frida enunciated. "And so do you." She pointed right at Emily's nose as the elevator came to a stop.

The doors opened and Frida launched into a long, boring story about oppression and poverty and corruption, but Emily was having a hard time following it.

She was standing in Megawoman's—her mother's—Super Palace. There were costume rooms and communication rooms and training rooms. Oh, and there were boots. Lots and lots of boots.

Frida just kept talking, following Emily from room to room. "Are you getting all of this?" she demanded. "Because I don't want to have to tell you again."

"Yes, yes." Emily waved her hand. "Someplace near Belize, spring break, Marvelous Cadillac whatever, blah, blah, blah." Frida scowled at her in the mirrored walls. But Emily could not bring herself to focus. She was too busy running her fingers over a pair of sequined thigh-highs. "My mother is Megawoman," she whispered to the

shiny footwear. It suddenly made sense to her, then, all of it: Her mother's ability to silence people with a look was the superdiluted version of the lethal withering look Megawoman was famous for. Her mother's fearlessness. Her independence. It was all part of being so much more than normal. . . .

"Your mother is very powerful," Frida confirmed, still frowning. "And so are you."

"I am?" Emily turned toward Frida then, batting her eyelashes and laying on some sugar. "Tell me more about me," she demanded. Without waiting to hear, she rushed to the training room they'd passed on the way. She'd tried to re-create her mother's powers. All of them. Any of them. But she wasn't able to so much as wilt a petunia with her glare. She had nothing.

Frida watched in silence, her dark brows knit together. "In time. In time," she finally murmured to Emily. But her worried expression remained. Then, perhaps because the longtime live-in knew Emily so well, Frida suggested the girl do a little "shopping" in her mother's closet. "It will cheer you up," she said. Emily couldn't deny it. Finding the silver number really had helped. If she couldn't stun somebody with a dirty look, she could at least look completely stunning.

"Your partner can help you develop your talents," Frida told her when they got back to the main level.

"My partner?" It took Emily a minute.

"Amanda is a good girl, stronger than you think," Frida insisted. "Stronger than you. Go talk to her. We need her help to save your mother . . . and hers."

Emily nodded and stepped up to the silly cottage door without flinching. She even rang the bell. But after that . . . The initial adventure had not gone very well, had it? Amanda had gone and knocked herself out in some dump and rendered Emily's current school experience a total nightmare. Not only was the entire student body all freaked out, but Vladimir or Virgil (or whatever unfortunate name that kid who hovered around Amanda had been given by his parents) was all up in her business. And worse, he had enlisted recruits.

The little wimp marched right up to Emily in the hall before lunch without a hint of shame. He stood at his full height of four feet eleven inches, barely reaching Emily's chin, and peered up at her face. "Is that an Olga of Antwerp Home Perm?" he shouted so everyone in the hall could hear. "I can smell it from here, and it looks"—he grimaced—"greasy." He waved his hand in front of his screwed-up face. "Clearly not a professional job."

Emily was taken aback by the shrimpboat's verbal assault on her naturally wavy hair. To make the situation more distasteful, he was flanked by no fewer than a half dozen other nerds wearing sensible footwear and headphones and toting laptops.

"Your glasses must have fogged," Emily answered, trying to remain calm. The hallway was not the place for a tantrum. "As if it's any of your business. And what would you know about *hairstyles*, anyway?"

"Please," Vincent snapped. "I know *everything* about hairstyles."

Emily served up her fiercest side-eye. The boy was unfazed. "Who said you could even talk to me?" she blurted. "And who are *those people*?" She waved a hand at his friends and wrinkled her nose.

"Look here, Mismatched Prints, I am trying to help you—Amanda told me everything. And *those people*"—the boy gestured to the pasty, breathless crew backing him—"are the fighting wing of Hack and Role, or as we prefer to be known, the Otaku Army."

Emily looked confused and the nerd leader leaned closer. "They're just some guys from the Robotics RPG Society. You know, in case you need backup," he added conspiratorially.

Emily felt her cheeks get warm. Of course Amanda had told the fragile boy everything. That was so like her. But Emily did *not* need backup. Certainly not from the Motley Order of Nerds Society. "Everything's fine. The

ROBOTICS RPG SOCIETY

Craig "Cheetos" Zatvatt, Arnix "Warp Speed" Detricklium, Prue "Slab" DeBona, Vincent "Kormar Mighty" Verbiglia, Stanislav "Butch" Poplovovich, Debra "Princess Le'Shera of Devrolax" Fund

last thing I want is a pack of brains on my tail." She gave the kid her *most* withering look, expecting him to retreat, but he stepped forward and lowered his voice instead.

"What do you mean, 'Everything's fine'? Have you even checked to see if Amanda's okay? Do you even care that The Exterminator, who is exacting some crazy revenge on your mothers, has poisoned her? No, you were too busy whining about getting a walnut shell enzyme scrub to worry about anyone but yourself."

How did he know about that? Emily's heart was pounding. The look of intensity on the little toady's face was unsettling, and she didn't want to admit her failure. She hadn't known for certain if The Exterminator was behind this business. She hadn't been brave enough to follow Amanda and find out.

"Last time I saw Amanda, she was at Armpit Acres," Emily blurted at the kid calling her out. "And for your information," she added smugly, "I'm the one who made sure she got out of there in one piece. One phone call from me, and she was on her way to safety. So stifle it, Sniffles, and get out of my way." She pushed past the pocket-size honor student, not-so-accidentally knocking him into the mob of goobers. The weaklings fell like bowling pins, cushioning their technology with their slacker bodies.

"Your skirt looks like it was sewn out of tablecloths!" the pint-size techie shouted after her as she stormed down the hall. "I saw those pleather shoes in the clearance bin at Pumps by the Pound," he added with glee. "Don't worry, no one can tell the difference."

Without even thinking, Emily punched her right hand directly into a locker. The metal door buckled and folded in on itself as if it were made of paper. She looked around— no one had seen her. No one but Amanda's friend, who stared at her with a small smile on his face.

By lunch Emily could stand it no longer. She walked off campus and all the way to Amanda's house. The route was ingrained in her memory from the days when the two girls used to walk there after free-form dance class at Ms. Bovinia's Jazz Danceteria and Crafts Cottage. That was back when they liked each other and had things in common. Both of them used to enjoy doing interpretive dance moves and making legume-and-noodle mosaics—

though their motifs differed. Emily preferred to create portraits and flowers with lentils and split peas, while Amanda invariably crafted something creepy and crawly out of pinto and black beans. Often she made bees.

"Ugh!" Emily squeezed her eyes shut.

Ever since they were toddlers, all Amanda ever talked about, or played, or was interested in were bees or grass-hoppers or other things with too many legs.

The memory now showing in Emily's head was a recollection from second grade. She had been practicing making French braids on her Enfant Terrible doll and wanted to discuss hair ties, but Amanda kept prattling on about bees. . . .

"Bees are amazing. They give it all. They devote their lives to the greater good. They're willing to sacrifice every-thing for the colony and their queen." Emily could swear that Amanda had wiped away tears as she herself had swal-lowed back bile. Bees gave her the heebies. Gross.

"Did you know bees only sting if they think their hive is threatened?" Amanda had gone on. And on. "They attack with their stingers, which are covered with spikes.

When they try to remove them, the barbs stick fast, like fishhooks, so then, when they try to fly away, they end up pulling out their own entrails—that's their guts—and they die! For the greater good!"

Just the memory of that sad speech made Emily queasy. But this time it wasn't because of the bee innards. It was because she knew Amanda was right. Amanda was the good one. The one willing to sacrifice. For others. For the greater good. Just like a bee.

As she stretched out her hand to ring the Prices' doorbell, Emily began to chicken out. She could not look into Amanda's grandfather's pale old eyes. He knew she had been out there with Amanda last night. He knew she had been more concerned about odors and clogged pores than Amanda's safety. And he probably knew that, unlike Amanda, Emily didn't have any real powers!

Emily stood for a moment longer on the front stoop, and then slipped around to the side yard. She couldn't face Poppy, but she had to know if Amanda was okay. She climbed the oak tree that grew past her old friend's window. She snagged her leggings and scraped her arms on her way up. She didn't care. When she got high enough to see inside, she almost wished she hadn't come at all.

Amanda was lying on her bed. She was covered in some sort of strange gossamer goo. The poor girl looked awful, more pale than ever. She wasn't moving . . . like, at all. *And what is that gunk?* Emily wondered, pursing her lips in distaste. It reminded her of some sort of creepy Silly String shroud, only shrouds were for dead people, and Amanda couldn't be—

Emily's thoughts were interrupted when the door to Amanda's bedroom creaked open. Poppy came into the room carrying a sewing basket. Emily tried not to move. She held tighter to the tree trunk and almost stopped breathing altogether.

Poppy looked worried. He paced a little before sitting down beside Amanda. He reached a hand toward his granddaughter, pulled it back, and used it to cover his mouth. Then, wordlessly, he picked a piece of green fabric out of the sewing basket and began to stitch.

HONEYBEE

Fun Bug Fact: Honeybees sting only as an act of defense. They also can kill an intruder wasp by covering the wasp in a ball of bees, increasing carbon dioxide and raising body temperature to lethal levels. This is called balling.

23

Oyster Cove Day dawned crisp and bright.

Nervous town dwellers everywhere turned on the news to see if the event of the year had been canceled and were quickly reassured that it would go on as scheduled. So, with trembling hands, people packed their picnic baskets and donned their shell-encrusted apparel.

Emily shut off her television. The news was totally bumming her out. Instead, she chose an insane decibel level for the inane pop playlist on her stereo and blasted it in her bedroom, hoping to drown out her own thoughts.

She'd been preparing for over an hour to tell Frida that there was NO WAY she was attending Oyster Cove Day—no matter how amazing the outfit she had selected was. She was "sick." Very, very sick. (At least that was her story, and she was sticking to it.) But she kept hearing voices in her head.

"You should be ashamed!" the voice scolded.

"Seriously, how could you *do* that?" the voice lambasted her. Emily winced.

The voice was not in her head.

The voice was in her room.

Pressing pause, Emily turned to see who had entered the sanctuary she'd ensconced herself in.

What she saw was not what she'd expected. Amanda's little friend was standing in the doorway of her bedroom. He was clad head to toe in lamé that was a dazzling shade of green and sporting a pair of mirrored goggles on top of a green leatherette aviator helmet.

"Kermit?" Emily asked, incredulous.

"Vincent!" Frida said loudly, stepping up behind the small boy with all the snappiness of a highly trained military officer. The faux housekeeper stood stone-still, flanking the Day-Glo boy and looking more than a little cranky. "This is *Vincent*, and he told me what you did," Frida growled. There was fire in her eyes. Emily had never seen her this angry before. It was impressive. It was easy to believe Frida could stare down nations.

But she was still in charge here, wasn't she? Frida was supposed to be on her side! Emily stood up and swallowed hard. "You mean he *told* on me?" She looked from Frida to Vincent. "You *told* on me?" she repeated. It was unbelievable. First the little brain dared speak to her, to *insult* her, and now he had ratted her out. Emily felt her face grow hot. Wasn't she having a bad enough week *already*?

"Amanda isn't getting any better," Vincent said quietly. "How could you have left her like that?" he asked. His eyes were red, and Emily realized the delicate child had been crying. *Oh no. Please don't let him cry here*, she silently begged, feeling her own eyelids grow warm.

Looking down and squeezing her eyes shut, Emily channeled every ounce of the fear and worry she was experiencing into an emotion she could deal with. Her anger flared hotter as she added to the list of Vincent's offenses: stood up to her, questioned her fashion and beauty choices, ratted her out, and *blamed* her for what had happened to Amanda. Emily opened her eyes and balled her hands into fists. This chartreuse munchkin couldn't blame her any more than she was already blaming herself!

"I didn't do that," Emily slowly enunciated.

"No!" Vincent fired back with more animosity than Emily would have believed possible. "You didn't *do* anything. You were too afraid of scuffing up last season's kicks to even *enter* the dump—which is exactly where those ugly shoes belong!"

Emily blinked. Her face felt like it was on fire. The mini frog kid must have been drawing some crazy courage from his costume to talk to her like that. He actually looked a little taller—perhaps there were lifts in his steel-toe boots.

"You didn't do anything *then*, but it's time you did something *now*." Vincent strode over to Emily's vanity and plopped down his laptop computer, which he then opened. On the screen was a live streaming image of the mysterious goings-on at Armpit Acres. A large circular area near the spot where Amanda had fallen was twitching and shifting like quicksand.

Suddenly, a tremendous boom shook the ground.

Frida crossed her arms over her chest, looked at Emily, and tapped her foot impatiently. She raised an eyebrow like, *Well?*

"See?" Vincent reproached Emily, too. He fixed her with a look.

"But what am I supposed to *do*?" Emily demanded, hoping she was the only one who heard the slight whimper in her voice. She didn't have antennae or armor or a withering gaze. All she had was good hair and teeth, a sick fashion sense, and an amazing outfit.

Vincent and Frida continued to look at her expectantly.

Emily felt helpless. Abandoned. Accused. And, and so, SO angry. *"What am I supposed to do?!"* she repeated in a furious shriek, squeezing her eyes shut.

The scream reverberated around the room. Crumbs of plaster fell on her head, and when she opened her eyes again, she saw Vincent, Frida, and the laptop all smashed against the opposite wall. Emily gasped and covered her mouth with her hands as they regained their footing.

"Something like that would be a good start," Frida said, dusting herself off. A tiny smile tugged at one corner of her mouth.

Vincent steadied himself and quickly checked that all his parts were intact. "But I think you need to direct that

energy over, uh, there." He gestured downwind, in the
direction of Armpit Acres. "Now."

Emily took her hand off her mouth. "Did I just do
that by—"

"Screaming, yes." Frida nodded and surveyed the mess.
"Let's take this outside."

Emily looked at the cracked wall. She looked down
at her hands. Her feet. She felt anger
still burning inside her. This was it!
This was her power. She DID have
power—fury! And she was so ready to
unleash it.

Well, almost ready. "One sec."
Emily held up a finger, darted into
the powder room, and returned
wearing a black mask that covered her eyes, her silver Lycra suit,
and a pair of puffy eighties aerobic
sneakers. "Now I'm ready."

Vincent nodded approvingly. "Sassy
unitard," he admitted.

Moments later, Emily was seated on Frida's aqua Vespa—Frida had insisted they take it and leave her to secure the house—speeding toward Armpit Acres with a Muppet of a boy clinging to her waist.

The sonic booms continued and dust filled the air, casting an evil hue over everything. But as they approached Armpit Acres, Emily noticed through the dust a different otherworldly glow seeping up from the trembling ground.

"That can't be good," she whispered to herself, slowing the scooter and waiting to see what would happen before getting any closer.

The ground shook as more of the bright glow shone through the rubbish. Then, like a UFO breaking free of its underground hangar, the form pushed away from the earth. The unidentified object had eight anchor points—four on each side—that it was using to hoist itself upward. With a jolt, the massive whatever-it-was tore itself free of its subterranean dwelling. Rubble spilled off the slanted sides, creating great waterfalls of waste. Vincent and Emily covered their mouths to keep from breathing the stench and possibly screaming.

Finally completely out of the ground, the giant glowing orb rested for a moment. Then, tentatively, it began to extend its mechanical legs to their full height and stood—a massive robotic arachnid—before them.

Multiple eyes gazed black and cold onto the landscape as the mechanical monster surveyed its target. All of Oyster Cove lay at its feet. Then, slowly, it began to walk. The glowing legs moved methodically over giant mounds of refuse and out onto the highway, where the machine began its unhurried march toward the city.

Emily felt like she was going to barf. She had no plan of action, really. She was just an angry kid in a figure-skating costume! What could she possibly do to this tank of a spider?

She was scared beyond belief, but she also knew that without Amanda and their mothers, she was the only being standing between this thing and the complete devastation of her hometown. She tried to muster up some of the passion she'd felt when she shriek-blasted Vinnie and Frida back in her room. She hadn't thought she was all that super then. Who knew what she might be able to muster up now that she was facing a real threat?

If Amanda could jump into a stinking pit, she could try to shriek this baby out of commission.

The enormous machine lumbered forward, ignoring the two defiant children racing after it on their scooter. The city streets were oddly quiet. Everyone was at Oyster Cove Day. As the robotic spider marched, its giant feet slammed down, leaving massive pockmarks in the street. The trail of terror resembled dots on a treasure map and led Emily and Vincent directly to the megabot's destination—the Science League Building.

The scooter slowed to a halt as the colossal spiderbot stopped, hovering over the alabaster dome of the huge building. Emily gulped. Breathing had become difficult.

"Okay, Frogger. What now?"

24

"**T**hrow something?" the kid in green suggested. "And get really mad!"

Good idea. Emily stepped off the scooter and spotted a rock-garden labyrinth resembling a petite Stonehenge. Ammo. She thought about people who tucked their sweaters into their jeans and felt her temperature rise. Then, with a motion so fast that she couldn't even process what her body was doing before she did it, she reached down to fling rock after rock at the giant metal spider.

Vincent cowered on the scooter, occasionally shouting insults to fuel her fury.

Emily narrowed in on a target—one of the spider's "eyes"—and began pummeling it with her precision projectiles. The large rocks tore through the air at amazing speed and made almost instant contact. They beat against the ocular glass dome in rapid succession. Glass shattered.

Lights flickered . . . the arachnid eye shot sparks and went dark. She had rendered it useless. Just like that.

"Huh," she said, as if she'd startled herself. She paused for a moment, making sure her unitard was unscathed, adjusted her bun, and stood up a little taller. "Not bad."

The demonstration of power made Emily feel a bit better. Even a bit *special*. In a good way. Her power was as real as Amanda's! And she was about to show the world!

"Um, Emily?" Vincent called out. He pointed at something over Emily's head, interrupting her moment of glory. "You might want to focus?" he suggested.

Emily jutted out a shiny hip and opened her mouth to tell Vincent not to tell her what she needed to *do* or *not do*. It was irritating. But she closed her mouth again when she looked in the direction he was pointing. The spider thingy was wheeling around to focus one of its still functioning "eyes" in her direction.

Emily dived behind the scooter with Vincent—there was no telling what kind of firepower that thing had. "Thanks," she said as they huddled together, then generously added, "Your outfit is totally cute, by the way."

Vincent blushed. Obviously he wasn't used to compliments. Certainly not from the überpopular.

The massive UFO-shaped spider dipped down as it swung back around, and Emily saw something inside one of the larger glowing eye domes she was not prepared for: Dragonfly and Megawoman!

The pair of supermoms was bound into seats behind the massive lens. Before the imprisoned heroes could see Emily, the spider spun again and straightened, lifting the women out of view.

"Vinnie, did you see that?" Emily choked out, clutching a handful of his synthetic suit. Every tiny hair on her body was standing at alert.

Her mother was inside that . . . thing.

Emily had been mad before. Plenty mad. But *never* had she felt as angry as she did now, seeing her mother frightened, defeated, and captive! Some old creep somewhere inside that contraption had kidnapped her mom—had taken from her the one person she was sure loved her no matter what—and was now torturing her by giving her a forced front-row seat to the destruction of the town she adored! That was not cool. That was not cool at all. Somebody was going down.

But knowing her mother was trapped inside the mechaspider, Emily was at a loss about how to proceed.

The spiderbot, which had been screeching terribly, suddenly went quiet. The silence was unnerving. Then Emily heard the crackle of a PA system followed by a hacking cough. Gross.

"Hello, child," a voice rasped.

Emily looked around.

"Yes, you in the silver suit," the voice said. Emily scowled. She did not care to be called a child. Or addressed over a loudspeaker.

"I should have known there would be two of you," the voice complained. "And you are just as annoying as your pesky friend. You must be another obnoxious addition to a pathetic gaggle of absolutely wretched, terrible people inhabiting this cesspit. When will it end?"

Emily's scowl deepened. A week ago she would have been peeved that this loser had called Amanda her friend. Not to mention all those other words he had strung together. But she was madder that this menace was the reason Amanda was . . .

Emily sucked in her breath. She could not think about that.

She steeled herself and glared up at the hunk of metal. The eye Megawoman and Dragonfly were in was still too high for her to see.

"You'd better watch what you say, Octobot!" Emily shouted. She didn't think the guy in the spider tank would be able to hear her, but apparently he could.

"Or what? You won't 'like' me? You'll throw rocks?" He chuckled. "Oh, boo hoo. By the way, who's the lepre-chaun? Surely he's not another member of the hero brood. He looks too . . . wan and feeble, as if the wind might carry him away."

Vincent scowled and tugged at his shimmery shirt.

"Oh, I'm so glad you have revealed yourself, you little goiter," the villain continued, turning back to his main tar-get. "You're amusing. And I wouldn't want you to miss out on this little reunion I have planned. Or all of the fun!" The Exterminator released a sickening wheeze. "By the

way, do you have a name for yourself yet? Tantrum Twerp, perhaps? The Silver Simpleton?" He paused to chuckle. "Oh, let's just keep things simple. How about Oaf?"

"Why don't you stop babbling and crawl on out of there and face me, you coward?" Emily demanded.

The laughing started again. "Not before I give your mommy her presents," The Exterminator cackled.

"Oh dear. This should be gruesome," Vincent mumbled. He could barely look. "This is the scene of The Exterminator's humiliation," he explained, gesturing toward the science building. "I bet he's set on wiping this place off the map."

Emily gazed up at the SLB, as people around town had taken to calling it. The landmark was constructed out of chiseled marble and was a famous destination for intellectual pilgrims.

"And now here we are," The Exterminator said through the loudspeaker so all could hear. "At the place where my reign of fabulousness was vanquished. If only you two gibbons had let my plan go into full effect, none of this preposterous business would ever have been necessary." He had to be addressing the kidnapped Mega-woman and Dragonfly.

"I'd be ruling the planet, and you would . . . well, you wouldn't be here getting on my nerves. Then again, you probably wouldn't be *anywhere*, if you get my drift. But that will be taken care of soon enough, I assure you. Now watch this!" The Exterminator's mic shut off with a fizzle and a pop.

The spiderbot's top whirred. Out of its sides slid two enormous metallic arms that looked like they belonged to one of Amanda's praying mantis pets. Emily peered closely at the appendages and saw that tracing the interior of each claw were what appeared to be hooks. The tip of each arm was flattened into a giant sledgehammer head.

Emily turned to Vincent, hoping for some sort of reassurance, but his face was frozen in fear.

Then, with a jolt, the bot sprang into action, slamming the newly revealed weapons down onto the top of the old building with unimaginable force. Slabs of stone rained down everywhere. The great building cracked and crumbled, its pillars giving way and its supports toppling.

Glass sprayed from broken windows as the building collapsed into rubble. The roof fell like a ten-ton soufflé, shooting dust and debris skyward. Priceless papers and documents drifted down to earth to rest with chunks of rock, destroyed furniture, and invaluable artworks that had been rendered valueless.

Not satisfied that he had destroyed the building, The Exterminator kept smashing and smashing until there was little left but powder. He had turned his mic back on so the heroes could hear his infantile cackling. "Yes! Beautiful destruction!" he screamed as his machine finally halted its fatal thrashing.

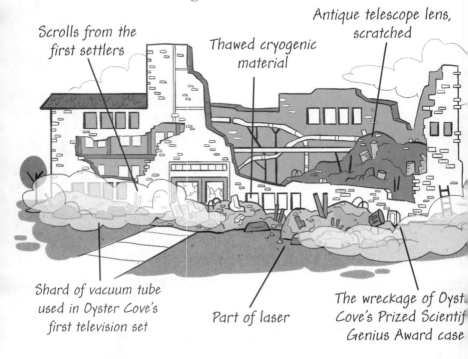

Scrolls from the first settlers

Thawed cryogenic material

Antique telescope lens, scratched

Shard of vacuum tube used in Oyster Cove's first television set

Part of laser

The wreckage of Oyst Cove's Prized Scientif Genius Award case

Emily and Vincent watched the spectacle from behind a large trash bin. Even with her new powers, Emily didn't think she could survive a hail of boulders. She was sure Vincent couldn't. As the dust settled, she peeked around the corner and saw the mantis arms retract back into their secret compartments. The spiderbot stood silently as if pondering the destruction that lay before it. Maybe The Exterminator just wanted to linger a bit to make sure Megawoman and Dragonfly had ample time to let what had just happened sink in. Emily couldn't be sure. But before she could decide what to do next, the giant machine turned and began to lumber up the street toward the town square.

The spider came to a standstill beside the courthouse. There was a noise like the flash warming up on an old camera, and then with a crack, a laser shot out of the spiderbot's mouth, exploding the city building. Then it fired a second beam, taking out the neighboring Natural History Museum.

"Um, Emily?" Vincent whispered, tugging at her elbow. "Lasers are a very advanced technology. I'd say we're pretty much outmatched at this point. We need to come up with an alternate plan of attack if we're to survive this skirmish."

Emily was not having it. "He can shove his advancements," she shouted, prancing forward. She would take this contraption out if it was the last thing she did.

She focused her attention on the legs of the creepy mech, possibly the weakest points of the armored vehicle. Then she lifted her foot and brought it down hard. The reverberations made the bot stumble. The walking machine wavered momentarily and regained its balance.

Emily stomped again. Cracks appeared in some of the nearby buildings, and the spiderbot struggled amid the tremors. The floundering robot began contracting its supports until the massive body was street level.

Emily ran closer, trying to catch a glimpse of her mother. She spotted her at last, and Dragonfly, too. Both of them were staring out of the lenslike window, but they weren't looking at Emily, or even the blasted buildings. Emily turned to see what could be more horrifying and let out a shriek.

A half dozen oversize locusts with glowing green eyes were touching down on the capitol lawn, bearing a large lumpy package between them. The mutant bugs backed away from the weird white bundle. And through the lacy covering, Emily made out a familiar face.

"Amanda!" Emily screamed. She charged toward the insects and her bound-up former friend. If those lame bugs had bothered to bring Amanda all the way out here, perhaps she was still alive . . . perhaps there was time to save her!

Emily was halfway across the lawn when one of the spiderbot's telescoping legs extended to reveal a pincer grip on the small end. Quick as a wink, the leg snatched Emily up and lifted her into the air.

"Let me go!" Emily hollered.

"Let her go!" Vinnie shrieked from the sidewalk.

Their protests were useless. Both of them watched helplessly as a second large leg extended, pinning the wrapped-up Amanda to the dirt. The Exterminator had captured them both.

25

Emily was a captive. She had never been so embarrassed in her entire life. . . . Imagine being caught by that old man! She could barely bring herself to look at the hunched-over creep as he directed his troops to lock her up inside one of the eyeballs of his enormous spiderbot. Seriously, the withered windbag looked too weak to move, much less take over a town! But, duh, that was why he'd created an army.

If it was just him, I could take him out, no problem, Emily consoled herself. But bound, gagged, and imprisoned in a ginormous spider tank, the spanking-new superhero could do nothing but stare out of her cell as The Exterminator maneuvered his great machine toward the edge of the Oyster Point cliffs.

Emily was not sure what The Exterminator had in mind once he reached the drop-off. But as the mechanical behemoth came to a stop on the ridge, idling sinisterly, she realized that from this vantage point she could see everything.

The Exterminator's attack weapon was deliberately poised so that the prison eye beside hers, the one containing Dragonfly and Megawoman, offered the trapped superheroes an uninterrupted view of the approaching chaos. It was the moment The Exterminator had been waiting for. And a moment Emily would not have conjured in her wildest nightmares.

Emily was separated from her mother and Mrs. Price, but she was not alone. The Exterminator had locked her in with Amanda—who had not so much as twitched since she was delivered to the big spider. The psycho scientist's weird soldiers had dumped the pair in the lockup while he watched. He'd coughed and cackled as they were deposited, calling the girls "an added bonus." Ugh. The last thing Emily wanted to be was the cherry on Craggy's sundae of vengeance.

That old crackpot was unbelievably creepy. Emily would have liked nothing more than to scream him out of existence, and she would have if he hadn't sealed her mouth shut with some putrid arachno-goo to stop what he called her "entitled whining." As if.

Luckily, The Exterminator hadn't captured Vincent. He'd sent one of his locusts to fetch him, but when Vinnie screamed and ran off squealing for "Poppy" and "Frida," The Exterminator called the drone off. "Never mind the infant in the green pajamas," he'd rasped. "Nothing to fear there. You two wretched little imps can just sit here and think about what you've done," he had seethed as the girls were installed in their eye prison. "Or not think. Your little friend there, what did she call herself? Bug Girl? She doesn't appear to be in a state that's capable of cognition. More like Slug Girl . . ." With that, he had clapped his hands together and leered, delighted with his zinger. Then his expression had changed back to distaste. "Horrid little girls. Oh. Just awful," he had muttered as one of his mutants spun a web of his world-famous unbreakable recipe tightly around Emily.

Emily could not wait for the gasbag to be gone so she could break out. Unfortunately, it turned out that The

Exterminator's web was as strong as he'd bragged. Emily was completely immobile. Even though she knew she looked good in her fabulous hero costume and mask, she was helpless. And Amanda . . . Emily tried not to think about Amanda's current state and was just a little bit glad that the other girl was lying behind her so she could not stare at her, searching for signs of life.

Squirming was getting Emily nowhere, and in fact it seemed to be tightening the bindings. So she lay still instead and contemplated what her next move could possibly be. Beneath her, she felt the giant contraption move. She writhed again, contorting her body so that she could see out the lens of the eye prison. Oh. This was not good.

The Exterminator's spider-bot was perched on the edge of the cliff overlooking the town's annual jamboree.

Oyster Cove Day was a community celebration, a joyous occasion looked forward

★ OYSTER ★
COVE DAY

Porky Pet Parade
Deviled-Egg-Eating Contest
Ham Toss
Hot Fudge Tidal Pool
Spin the Donkey
Frog Jump
Egg Hurdle
Clam Bake
Petting Zoo

Plus, blue ribbons for the town's finest specimens of produce, jam, noodle macramé, pie, shrubbery arrangement, bonsai beards, and more!

to by all. Usually. Today it looked more like a horror movie. Emily saw far below the terrified citizens of Oyster Cove shuffling around like paranoid zombies. Alas. No lawn darts were being tossed, no petting-zoo animals were being stroked and fed nubs of corn, no children were hyper on cotton candy, and no clams were being potted up for baking. It appeared that even the popular Hot Fudge Tidal Pool was empty.

Squinting into the distance, Emily thought she recognized some of her classmates in the crowd. Lars Viddlehammer and Stacy Waxenblough were cowering against the entrance to the Horror House. Annie Mismeadows was curled in a ball, her eyes poking up above her knees, looking very much like one of the mollusks in the Crack-a-Clam game she was huddling against.

Emily looked away from the celebration and sighed, realizing that her dream of debuting her new (and absolutely perfect) outfit would not come true. But her dramatic exhalation caught in her throat when she saw what was happening in the sky before her. It was something far more terrible than fashion woes. It was something that made Emily reel in horror.

The spider was launching an army.

Somewhere over Emily's head, giant bay doors had opened, ejecting insect monstrosities. The same locusts that had dragged Amanda to The Exterminator's mobile lair were now floating high above Oyster Point, carrying in their legs what looked like giant egg sacs. *Ugh, bugs.* Emily shuddered. *Why is it always bugs?*

The beasts lingered at attention, their ranks stretching the length of the cliff, awaiting their creator's commands.

Below the wretched throng, Emily watched the Ferris wheel spinning lazily and the rickety roller coaster scuttling along its tracks. The muffled screams of shaken riders reminded her that citizens, terrified or not, were in fact at the festival, which meant there were more people in danger. And she was helpless to warn them.

Emily cringed when the spiderbot issued a near-deafening hiss and crackle. The Exterminator was about to make another one of his psychotic proclamations.

"Hear ye, hear ye!" the speaker burbled.

All Oyster Cove Day action ceased, and people turned to gaze up. Not sure what to think, they just stood and stared. Frozen by fear.

"Now that I've finally got your attention," The Exterminator snarled, "I'll tell you what's about to happen. Oh, you drab, tiresome little people. You are in for such a spectacular treat! For you see, I, The Exterminator, am about to take all of you prisoner, make you my slaves, and throw you into servitude for the rest of your lives, where you will do my bidding or face extreme consequences!" He started to cackle but was interrupted by a combination of gas bubble and cough.

Emily momentarily forgot her plight and rolled her eyes.

"You people laughed at me. You stole my livelihood. You mocked me. You called me mad. Mad? I'll show you mad! Now that I have the upper hand, I'm going to make you all pay for doubting my research! Ha!"

The crowd continued to stare, unmoving, at the cliff and the mechanical horror perched on it surrounded by locusts hovering in place.

"Oh, and by the way," The Exterminator continued,

"you needn't bother attempting to contact the outside world for help, for you are quite literally trapped here and"—he paused for effect as a green burst pulsed from the spiderbot's central eye through the crowd—"your cellular devices and modes of communication have just been disrupted. You are completely at my mercy!"

The locusts buzzed closer to the fair. Emily watched the horrors zooming through the clouds, clutching egg sacs close to their abdomens. Once the mutant bugs were close enough to the carnival, they dropped their eggs like bombs, careening down into the masses. When the sacs landed, they burst open and unleashed scads of colossal hybrid centipedes, beetles, and scorpions. The creatures budded like flowers of doom, squirmed into consciousness, and began their rampage. The horrors scuttled throughout the fair wielding pincers and stingers, sending the townspeople screaming for their lives.

Scared citizens grasped their children and fled, diving under tents, scurrying through

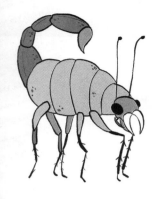

fences, scrambling toward the water, and even hiding beneath animals in the petting zoo. One mother hurled her toddler directly into the Hot Fudge Tidal Pool before joining him. Covered in liquid chocolate, they hoped to be invisible.

"Where is Dragonfly?" one man cried, barely avoiding being clamped in a bright green scorpion's pincers. "We need help! Where is she?"

"And where is Megawoman?"

Others in the crowd soon joined in the cry, as if bemoaning their near-forgotten heroes' absence would make them appear out of the ether.

Emily struggled to speak. She wanted to scream, "They are right here, you sniveling wusses! And maybe this time it's your turn to save *them*, and while you're at it, save *me*!" But her fidgeting only caused the binds holding her to tighten. If they constricted much farther, she wouldn't be able to breathe.

Emily was tempted to close her eyes and block out the scene before her. But she could not tear herself away.

All the while, The Exterminator cackled through the mic, enjoying the hysteria.

"Dear fools," he purred, "I am delighted to let you know that your precious heroes Dragonfly and Mega-woman won't save you this time. I've taken care of everything! My nightmare monsters lured them out of seclusion—and allowed me to capture them quite handily. You never even considered that it was I behind those delicious holographic attacks . . . and your 'heroes' didn't, either—until it was too late! Simple, dim Dragonfly and her little fashion-forward partner fell for my plan like eager, senseless preschoolers," he guffawed.

"Well, now we've all had our fun on Oyster Cove Day, and the Final Phase of my plan shall go into effect. Your lives are all about to be changed . . . permanently."

Emily's eyes were wide with terror. She saw that the centipedes had formed a ring around the entire basin. No one would be able to pass without getting bitten. The locusts still hovered over the crowd holding more egg sacs, should the need for backup arise.

The spiderbot rose higher on its many legs and shone

a red beam down on the fair. The beasts on the ground took in what must have been a silent command from their demented leader. Each creature, aside from the centipede guards, lifted up on its hind legs and snatched the human closest to it and held tight. The red beam continued to pulse until The Exterminator was sure that each Oyster Covian, right down to the youngest child, had been seized by one of his creations.

"And now, my dear Oyster Cove," The Exterminator blathered into his precious microphone, "you will take up your new duties in my mass-production facility. You will help me create a mega-army that will take over the country, and then . . . the world!"

26

Emily didn't like this new icky feeling of defeat. Things always went her way, and if they didn't, she'd had means of *making* things go her way. But in this situation, she was stumped.

She wondered what her mother was going through in the next cell. Her frustration had to be worse. All those years of protecting Oyster Cove, only to be forced to witness the community being destroyed in front of her eyes. Emily felt terrible for her mother and Amanda's as well. If they ever got out of this, Emily promised that she would thank them both for all they had done.

Right now, though, escape was a very big *if*. And it seemed as if it was about to get bigger.

A rumble shook the earth, and gargantuan beetles poured forth, revealing a cavernous pit. Emily shuddered.

Near the yawning cavern, the other hybrid monsters

had released their captives, forcing the Oyster Covians into a single-file line. It appeared the entire population of the town was about to be marched into this pit of misery.

Watching the parade of shame, Emily had a brief glimmer of hope—with luck, it wouldn't be too long before outside help came to save them. Another thought immediately followed: How would anyone know where to look for them if they were all underground? The situation was completely unacceptable and made Emily want to cry.

The townspeople felt similarly. They stood with their heads down, defeated and sad. The children trembled as they clutched their parents' legs or wrapped their arms around their guardians' necks.

A siren blasted. Not a good sign, and Emily surveyed the situation, bidding farewell to her last shred of hope. But wait. She saw something. Or thought she did.

A flash of green behind the sno-cone vendor's cart made her heart rate increase. Her gaze remained fixed on the spot until she saw a second verdant shimmer. Yes! Vincent and his nerds were down there, working desperately on their laptops. Somehow they had eluded capture and

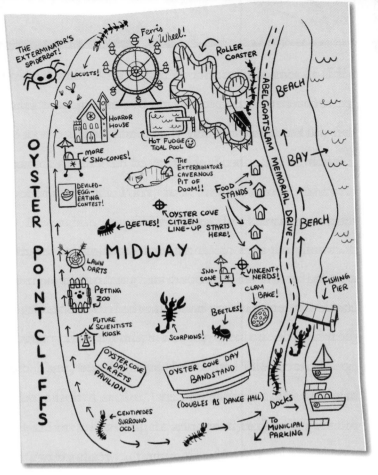

figured out a way to bypass The Exterminator's device disruption! They were tapping away, their heads bobbing up every few seconds to check the situation.

From her prone spot on the floor, Emily could see two of the science enthusiasts scampering away from their group holding what looked like makeshift receivers. They rushed around the perimeter of the centipedes, sneaking

behind carnival tents, popcorn stands, and hay bales to reach their appointed locations. In position, they lifted their DIY contraptions into the air and waited.

Behind the cone, Vincent raised his hand in a countdown so the other brains would know when to act. Five, four, three, two, ONE!

Emily couldn't see anything happening but heard a crackle like a transformer blowing out. And although she couldn't understand exactly what the nerds had done, she saw the results. She had to give it to Vincent. He was a smarty.

Whatever Vinnie and the Hack and Rolers engineered made the bug army shake their heads as if trying to rid themselves of bad memories, flailing and gyrating like modern dancers. And by the time they regained control, their prisoners had scrambled away.

Emily wanted to cheer. Vincent and his cronies had given Oyster Cove a fighting chance! Except . . . the centipede things ringing the lot of them hadn't been affected. The experiment had only worked on the mutant insects and arachnids. But she hoped it would be enough.

The superhero was so absorbed with watching what

was going on outside that at first she didn't notice the faint glow coming from within her cell. It pulsated more and more brightly, filling the prison room with yellow light before fading back to darkness.

When Emily finally noticed the shifting light, she was too terrified to guess what was happening behind her; she feared it was another monstrous bug sent to finish her off.

The light grew in intensity. Soon it was accompanied by a scratching noise that sent chills down Emily's spine. If she'd been able to turn her head to look, she wasn't sure she would have had the courage.

But finally she heard what sounded like a sheet being ripped in half and saw a puff of luminous, glittering dust filling the air around her. In the glow, it looked like New Year's Eve.

She heard loud breathing. Something behind her was gulping in massive amounts of air.

And then a blur shot past her and burst right through the glass of the spiderbot's eye.

Bug Girl was back!

27

Amanda awoke from what must have been a really deep slumber to an urgent alarm buzzing in her head. Something of massive importance was going on, and she needed to help. But what was it, and where the heck was she? With a power and drive she had never felt before, she literally ripped off her covers and launched herself up without taking so much as a second to figure out what was happening. There was a crash. A scream. A thud. And . . .

Amanda shook her head. This was not her bedroom! She stood still for a moment and looked around. She was standing on the beach. On what was obviously Oyster Cove Day . . . only, it was Oyster Cove Day gone horribly wrong!

"What the heck?" Everywhere Amanda looked, she saw giant beetles and scorpions and centipedes rushing around acting kooky. It would have been her dream. (Bugs!

Big, beautiful bugs!) Only these bugs were abnormal and not acting very nice at all.

Amanda blinked and squeezed her eyes shut for a second. She fought to recall all that had transpired before her strange nap and realized in a rush who must be behind the mutant bugs: The Exterminator. Of course. The crazy things running amok were the hybrid experiments he'd created for his little takeover plot. And somehow she had woken up in the middle of a full-on attack.

Amanda reached up to transform her headband into a mask and then spun slowly to take everything in. She looked up and saw an enormous spiderbot perched on the edge of the cliff above it all—it had to be The Exterminator's mobile-command center. Several of the bot's "eyes" were shattered. Apparently the battle she'd just joined had been going on for a while! Although the bot was damaged, it appeared to be functional. She was definitely going to have to take that tank out. But first she had to make sure the citizens were safe.

"Go, Bug Girl! Kick them in their hybridized insecto-trochanters!" a familiar voice shouted. Amanda turned to see a figure clad head to toe in dazzling green lamé standing next to the churro booth.

"Vincent?" she gasped.

"Present." Vincent Verbiglia jogged over, handed Amanda a churro, and stood before her like he was reporting for duty.

"Wow," she said, looking her friend up and down. The ensemble Vincent was sporting was BOSS. From the shining boots to the verdant aviator-like helmet (and goggles). "Wow."

Vincent shrugged. "I know. I made it myself," he said proudly. "With a little sewing guidance from your grandfather."

"It's amazing. You're so talented! So, can you fill me in on what's going on here? From the look of things, I missed quite a bit." She jammed most of the churro into her mouth and chewed while she waited for the update.

Vincent was silent, and Amanda realized he was staring at her, like, *really* staring, completely agog. He hadn't heard a single word she'd said to him after "Wow."

"Um, hello? Vincent?" She snapped her fingers.

"Uh, Amanda, I'm, uh, sorry but . . . it's just . . . you've . . . changed. I mean, you're different. You might want to take a look." Vincent had an expression on his face that was hard to describe. Awe? Horror? Amanda had basically just rolled out of bed. She couldn't imagine how bad her bed-head must be to make Vincent stare like that.

She wiped the cinnamon and sugar off her mouth, looked down, and gasped. This wasn't about a bad hair day. Her entire body was encased in a new exoskeleton—like her old one, but turned up to eleven! It shone exquisitely and was slickly metallic and shimmered with those cool rainbows that show up on soap bubbles and oil slicks. She turned her leg, watching the colors change. It was amazing, like a Japanese beetle. She hadn't just been asleep. . . .

"I thought you were dying!" Vincent practically sobbed with relief. "But you were in a cocoon! You were metamorphosing!"

"Say, this sure is glamorous." Amanda beamed. She looked fierce. And she felt even fiercer. "But we'll have to admire it later. You need to tell me what's going on. And then I need to take that old jerk down. He's probably up there laughing at us!" She pointed up at the cliff.

Vincent rattled off the latest, waving his arms back and forth, recounting all that had happened. He let her know that as a last-ditch effort, he and the Hack and Rolers had modified his Future Scientists Kiosk experiment to create a makeshift negative electric charge that had freaked out the insects and arachnids. It had worked . . . temporarily. But it hadn't affected the centipedes, and now the other crawlers seemed to be back under The Exterminator's control again and were chasing terrified citizens around the beach.

"Right," Amanda huffed. "First I'm going to have to knock these bad bugs out!"

As the words slipped out of her mouth, Amanda heard a buzzing noise overhead. She looked up just in time to see three of the locusts dropping eggs. The living bombs plopped on all sides and released fresh batches of foes. Vincent shrieked and ran. Flashy hero costume or not, he wasn't cut out for combat, and he knew it. He would be of more help from the sidelines.

"Good luck, Bug Girl!" he screamed to his friend as he regrouped with the nerds.

The monsters swarmed around her, but the out-numbered sixth grader showed no fear. That was the old Amanda. This was Bug Girl! She let loose blasts from her tymbals that sent the mad-science creepies flying left and right. Her sonic powers had been amplified during her big nap. Now they were strong enough to blow the bugs away. By the time she finished, the pile of twitching thoraxes and spasming body segments was taller than she was.

"Help! Help me!" Bug Girl heard someone scream behind her. She leaped up over the mound of fallen bugs and saw Calypso Jade being pursued by a small legion of large scorpions.

Bug Girl rushed closer. Calypso was barely keeping ahead of the scampering scorps, but she was trying her hardest. As she overtook the group, Bug Girl flipped up and over the giant arachnids and landed between them and Calypso.

The trembling socialite stood and gawked for a sec-ond before hightailing it, leaving Bug Girl standing on the fishing pier with seven enormous scorpions before her. "Seriously?" Bug Girl called after her. "No 'thank you'?" The scorpions' stingers were all arched overhead, ready to strike, and their claws were opened in full attack mode. She was cornered.

"Oh . . . so not good." Bug Girl fidgeted. She was brave, but she was not stupid. She turned and ran, figuring she could jump into the water to get away if she had to. She was a good swimmer, and she was betting the giant arachnids weren't. Close behind her she heard the clacks of their claws snapping. How were these things so quick? She was running faster than she had after Emily's party, *faster than Olympian Goddess speed*, faster than ever before, yet they seemed to be keeping pace. Just a few more yards, and she'd be in the water. She prepared herself for impact and took a giant gulp of air as she ran right off the edge of the pier!

Bug Girl braced.

But there was no impact. She heard the scorpions splash down into the bay one by one and looked down.

She wasn't even close to the water! In fact, she was

actually higher than she had been before she'd jumped off the pier.

Bug Girl was flying!

"Amazing!" she heard Vincent shout in the distance. "Bug Girl, you're amazing!"

Bug Girl felt . . . amazing. And unusually light. She heard a strange hum resonating behind her and turned to see just what was going on back there. What she saw made her suck in her breath. One of the locusts was zooming toward her, snarling crazily. But more shocking than that was the enormous pair of iridescent wings holding her aloft. Wings. *Her* wings.

Below her, Oyster Point was getting smaller and smaller as she climbed higher and higher.

And then, right there in midair, with the maniacal beast still in pursuit, Bug Girl took a moment. She looked at herself gliding through the sky—she was radiant in the sunlight. Even more amazingly, she had sprouted wings and she knew how to use them! Her see-through flappers were beating faster than a hummingbird's, keeping her just out of range of her attacker.

They were miraculous.

Bug Girl could not believe she could do something like this so naturally, like an insect taking its first flight. It was . . . instinctual. And she hadn't even dared to hope that her powers would include something as radical as flight.

She hovered for a split second and then boldly turned to face the leviathan roaring after her. She launched herself directly at it with fists extended, planning to make contact with this jerk and send it spiraling into the ocean to meet up with its nasty friends.

She connected with the monster at full power, but it didn't scream and it didn't fight back. It just burst into a spray of powder like a puffball fungus. There wasn't anything to it!

Bug Girl surveyed the sky. There were eight or nine more of these things fluttering around with sacs ready to drop. She had to take them out.

Bug Girl sailed swiftly through the air, pounding each flapping trooper and sending the eggs out to the sea, where they landed with a plop. Orange dust from the locusts drifted down onto the sand.

Having vanquished the suppliers of new insectile infantry along with their deadly eggs, Bug Girl touched down next to Vincent to catch her breath.

"Z-zowie," Vincent stammered. "I have never been so jealous of a single human being in my entire life. You can fly!" He circled around her to look at her wings, but they were now safely tucked back under their elytra. "Where'd they go?" Vincent demanded.

"I don't know how to turn them on yet." Bug Girl shrugged. "I guess I just have to run and jump, and they'll open up—a theory I'll get to test, like, any second now."

At that, Vincent started jumping up and down excitedly. "Oh my gosh, oh my gosh!" Vincent yelled, waving his arms up and down as if he were trying to fly, too. "I totally forgot to tell you something really important! When you burst out of that eyeball thing up there, you left Emily inside. She's trapped in that spider . . . and so are your mothers!"

28

Bug Girl's jaw dropped. Her mother was within her grasp, directly above her on the cliff. In the big spider mech! And she could save her!

Bug Girl looked around. Hundreds of people were in need of immediate help. Yes, she had annihilated the air locusts and the army's ability to grow, but who knew what other tricks The Exterminator had up the sleeve of his lab coat?

She needed to get up to the fogey's base and free Emily and their mothers. Together, the four of them would be unstoppable against this toad and his ghouls.

"Vincent, I need you to wait here," Bug Girl ordered.

"Um, okay." The boy nodded. He stood back and watched in awe as Bug Girl sprinted forward and jumped into the air. Her first attempt was a dud. She landed on the sand and looked sheepishly back at Vincent.

"I didn't say anything," Vincent protested. "I'm just jealous. Now get up there!"

Bug Girl took a deep breath before launching a second attempt. She exhaled, clenched her hands into fists, and propelled herself forward until she was running full tilt. She took a few tenuous hops, but nothing clicked. Finally, she dug deep into her brain and pictured her mother, helpless, held prisoner by that demented goat with the revolting dentition. Then, with one final leap, she felt her wings splay outward from beneath their protective coverings and begin beating. She had done it! She was zooming straight up toward The Exterminator's base of ops.

Nestled on the edge of the cliff, the spiderbot hadn't moved. Bug Girl flew back through the hole she'd burst out of earlier and found Emily glued in position, her eyes wide with surprise. And envy. Amanda totally knew what Emily was thinking: *Why can't I fly?*

Skidding to a halt, Bug Girl knelt beside her reluctant partner. She tugged at the binding threads, but she could not snap them. The web was unbreakable!

In order to save their mothers, Bug Girl was going

to need Emily's help. Her frustration grew, and so did a gurgling in her gullet, not like she was hungry but like something was churning inside her—gastric liquids from two separate locations. The gurgling subsided briefly, and she began to fidget. What was going on? Was she about to explode? Again she felt the bubbling.

Instead of totally freaking out, Bug Girl considered the possibility that this was another amazing insect power manifesting itself. The bombardier beetle, when threatened, mixed two chemicals produced within its own body and shot the hot, toxic concoction as a defense. That could be what was happening to her. She hoped.

The bubbling rippled through her again. She felt the chemical combo swirling in her abdomen. Once the compounds mixed, they heated up to a ridiculous temperature—surely she would be burning alive right now had she not gone through her ... um, changes. Suddenly the mixture shot out of her mouth in a controlled burst, hitting the wall behind Emily. And, *ew*. It tasted really bad.

Bug Girl coughed and spat and looked over at where the compound had landed. Sure enough, the biochemical cocktail had burned a sizable hole in the wall, with smoke rising from the edges. This stuff meant business!

"Okay, Emily, I'm going to get you out of there. But whatever you do, promise me right now that we are never going to talk about it. Do you promise?" Emily attempted to move her head. "I'll take that as a yes."

Gurgling again, Bug Girl felt a new batch of chemicals brewing. She had to be careful not to burn Emily.

Bug Girl took aim and spat small blobs of burning, acidic juice directly onto the strands that held Emily tight. The cords sizzled and smoked and slowly began to dissolve. With impressive precision, she dissolved more and more of the sturdy fibers.

Emily pulled her arms apart forcefully, and the bindings yielded at last. A few carefully placed spitballs on the webbing around Emily's head, and she was free! Emily reached up to clear her mouth. Bug Girl waited for the gratitude she was sure would follow.

"That was completely gross." Emily shuddered.

"I told you not to talk about it!" Bug Girl grumbled.

"Well, it was gross, but . . . thank you," Emily added,

rubbing her wrists and kicking her legs to get the blood flowing again. "I never thought I'd be saved by loogies."

"For your information, that was not a *loogie*. It was a defense mechanism that wards off predators," Bug Girl corrected, slightly hurt.

"Okay, okay!" Emily dismissed the conflict and pointed outside. "Let's not fight. We've got to get to that other eye and save our moms!"

For the first time, Amanda looked over and saw her mother and Emily's bound in the next cell.

But before the duo had the chance to make a move, the spiderbot lurched. Emily lost her footing and slid down toward the gaping window. She scratched at the smooth floor, unable to get a grip. The giant machine heaved again, pitching forward and sending the two girls right through the broken eye and over the edge of the cliff.

Emily shrieked hysterically, flailing her arms. She was careening toward the beach, falling faster and faster . . . about to slam right into the ground!

BOMBARDIER BEETLE

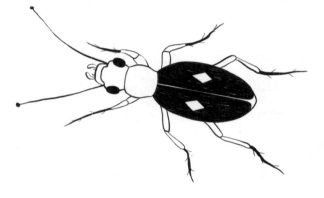

Fun Bug Fact: The bombardier beetle has a defense mechanism that allows it to spray noxious chemicals from its abdomen. The beetle has two reservoirs of chemical compounds inside that react together to create heat and gas, which drive the eruption of its spray.

29

Bug Girl grabbed Emily and the two girls glided through the air to the beach, Bug Girl's wings folding into place as they touched down.

Bug Girl looked at Emily as they landed in the sand. Emily looked like she wanted to hit something. She looked like she wanted to sprout her own wings. Or maybe rip Bug Girl's off.

"Those are stunning," Emily finally said, pointing to the hero's latest appendages. Then she swallowed and made a face—the combination of Exterminator glue and pride was foul, but she kept it down. "Thank you *again*, Amanda," she mumbled.

"You're welcome. And call me Bug Girl," she chirped back. She knew this wasn't easy for Emily. But she kind of liked it. "Now, what's our plan?"

The two girls looked up at the teetering spiderbot at

the same time. They needed to save their mothers—and get some help. Dragonfly's crushing powers would be superhandy in decimating the beach bugs. And Megawoman would be able to wipe out swarms of them with her patented withering stare.

"Get me back up there," Emily barked, pointing at The Exterminator's hub.

Bug Girl linked arms with the silver-clad girl and ordered her to run. "Faster," she barked. The attempted takeoff wasn't pretty. Two more awkward tries and Amanda could feel her lungs and cheeks burning.

"Sorry, this is kind of new to me," she apologized.

"Never apologize," Emily said. "You're stronger than you think."

Surprised by Emily's praise, Bug Girl smiled gratefully. "How about I lift off first and come back for you?"

"Great. But do it now." Though the pair had landed pretty far from the mayhem occurring at the festival, a few of The Exterminator's mutant army had spotted them and were making their way over on waaaay too many legs.

Bug Girl took off like a pro without the extra weight.

She swooped back around low and grasped Emily under the arms, and the pair was airborne. They were gaining altitude when out of nowhere came a new threat. Horrid multicolored wasps dove down to attack them, emitting a deranged percussive screech. There was no way Bug Girl could maneuver through so many new menaces. She touched down on the beach with the intention of beating the bad bugs at their own game.

"Let's show these jerks," Emily shouted, Bug Girl at her side. Together they unleashed a battery. Bug Girl blasted the wasps with her sonic powers—her tymbals were infinitely more powerful than theirs—while Emily hurled rocks and insults.

"Nasty gnats!" Emily screeched, taking down two with one stone. "Creepy crawlers!" She took out another.

Bug Girl upped her energy and, with a final lungful of air, blasted the remainder of the buzzers out of the sky. "Wimpy wasps, more like," she retorted.

"Bugs." Emily shuddered. "No offense."

"None taken." Bug Girl nodded. "Nice arm."

Suddenly the screams and cries of the crowd at Oyster

Cove Day increased in pitch and fervor. The young heroes turned to look down the beach.

"Looks like our moms are going to have to wait," Bug Girl shouted, grabbing Emily and dragging her closer. "The people of Oyster Cove need our help *now*!"

"But there are so many of those nasty things!" Emily shouted back. "How can we stop them?"

Bug Girl paced on the sand. "Let's start with the beetles. If we flip them over on their backs, they can't get up!"

"Wait." Emily stopped and stared at Bug Girl. "You mean, touch them? Can't we just get a giant can of Spray-a-Bug or something? Besides, they're not all beetles. What about those things with the stingers and those ugly ones with, like, nine million legs?"

Bug Girl was momentarily stunned by the fact that Emily knew the difference between insects, arachnids, and myriapods. Perhaps she had been doing more than braiding her dolls' hair all the years that they were friends. Perhaps she'd been listening.

"You're right," Bug Girl started to say as one of the giant bugs lumbered over to her. "Karate chop!" Bug Girl

INSECTS

- Three body parts: head, thorax, abdomen
- Six legs
- May have wings
- One pair of compound eyes
- Two antennae

ARACHNIDS

- Two body parts: abdomen, cephalothorax
- Eight legs
- No wings
- One to six pairs of simple eyes
- No antennae

shouted as she demonstrated a dazzling insecto-tackle. In no time flat, the bug was down, its legs kicking. Finally realizing it was helpless, it stopped moving.

"Okay! Here's what we'll do," Bug Girl said to Emily. "You and I will take care of the scorpions and centipedes. We can get everyone else to work together to put the insects on their backs. Teamwork!"

"Teamwork," Emily repeated, bracing herself for the ickiness. "I'll touch them. And when this is over, I'm taking the longest bath in the history of the universe."

Bug Girl inhaled deeply.

"Everyone!" she shouted authoritatively, addressing the panicking crowd. "We need your help to defeat The

Exterminator's army! Work in teams to flip the giant beetles over, like this one here." She pointed at the sad excuse for a mutant that was still idle on its back. "My partner and I will wipe out the big, ugly, nasty ones. Then we'll bring that geezer to justice and return Megawoman and Dragonfly to Oyster Cove!" There was a small, frightened cheer. "I want to see you ALL working," Bug Girl ordered, striking a heroic pose, hands on hips, just for a moment. Then she punched the air and added, "Let's go!"

Tentatively at first, but then with what looked like growing enthusiasm, the people of Oyster Cove turned on the bugs that had been chasing them. Soon the entire beach was a rush of bug-flipping fanatics, some keeping count of their victories, but all cheering as each new mutant was flipped and rendered immobile.

Meanwhile, Emily and Bug Girl started in on the arachnids and myriapods. Emily hurled Oyster Cove trophies, giant vegetables, homemade jams, and Skee-Balls—anything she could get her fiercely accurate hands on—at the beasts. But the frenzied crowd of beetle flippers was getting in her way.

Bug Girl zoomed overhead, her wings a blur—but she wasn't sure how to knock the scorpions out with her tymbals without also blasting bystanders. Her tentative blasts only seemed to be angering the creeps and making them scramble madly after her, stingers pointed skyward.

Bug Girl felt through her antennae that Emily was trying to get her attention. She looked down and saw the silver girl pointing toward The Exterminator's sinkhole workshop. *Good idea.*

"Okay, let's show these fools who's boss," Bug Girl shouted, racing earthward.

Working quickly, Bug Girl landed on the beach. She mercilessly teased and taunted each and every mutant with eight legs or more until they were all pursuing her. "Come on, you chilopodic creeps!" she shouted. "You, too, arachnidic chumps!" When she was certain that every single one was focused on wiping her out, she led them Pied Piper–style toward the crater and began circling.

With the mutants all surrounding Bug Girl on the edge of the pit, Emily stormed over. Then the angry super–sixth grader put her foot down. Emily stomped again and again, throwing a temper fit the likes of which had never been seen before.

The massive hole began to collapse, sucking the mutants into it like sand through an hourglass. Gone and buried. To make extra sure there was no chance the creeps would resurface, Emily compacted the dirt with several ultrapowerful jumps.

The Oyster Cove Day celebrants were silent for a moment; then they burst into a momentous cheer. People stood, dusted themselves off, and began shaking hands. Emily and Bug Girl walked to the center of the throng, and the ovation grew louder. With the bugs on their backs and the rest of the mutations underground, it seemed like the day had been saved.

Then a speaker crackled.

"Ugh," Bug Girl and Emily groaned in unison.

Chunks of rock and debris rained down from the cliff as The Exterminator's giant contraption pulled itself to standing. Light leaked from the seams in the hull, and with a sonic boom, the outer shell split off to reveal a smaller, sleeker ship—an escape pod within.

The smaller craft was black as obsidian and glistened in the late-afternoon sun. Its engine roared to life, and it blasted off into the sky. After a brief aerial tour of the damage, the craft hovered over the heroic girls, who were rolling their eyes. They could sense a speech was coming.

"Testing, testing. Is this thing on? Oh good, it's working again," The Exterminator spat into his microphone as his escape craft hovered over the frenzied masses below.

"Oh, you insufferable children," The Exterminator's voice blurted over the loudspeaker. "Just look at what you've done to my beautiful plan. No matter. I've still got your mothers. And if I'm going to lose, then so are they! You see, children, I've just activated what would be called Phase Three of my Sinister Plan—or was it Phase Four? Oh, I can't remember. It's a contingency phase, anyway, which I hadn't expected to have to bring into play. But since you ghastly things have defeated my beautiful army, it looks like I have only one option left."

Emily and Bug Girl glanced at each other. This wasn't going to be good.

"I'm going to detonate this ship and take Megawoman,

Dragonfly, you two foul little urchins, and every other disgraceful troglodyte in Oyster Cove with me! Then we'll see who was right all along. And in case you're wondering, the answer is me. The world will have me to thank when they are rid of this horrid town with its ice cream socials and pumpkin-carving contests and contra-dancing festivals and quilting bees. Disgusting!"

The black saucer touched down on the beach, and a computerized voice began a countdown. They had only sixty seconds!

There was no time to think or plan. Emily raced over to the contraption and, bracing herself beneath its hind end, pushed up with all her might. She groaned and screamed but managed to lift the ship up above her head. Her knees shook with the effort. In fact, her whole body quaked. It looked to everyone on the beach as if she might actually be crushed beneath the weight of the explosive escape craft!

"Your outfit is completely unflattering!" Vincent screamed from behind a group of terrified Oyster Covians. Emily's legs grew still.

"Where did you get it, at the Thrif-T Bargain Barn?" he yelled disgustedly.

Several people in the crowd glared at Vincent. How dare he heckle a hero? But Bug Girl knew what he was doing and grinned.

"You look like a baked potato!" he hollered.

That did it. With supernatural strength, Emily sent the disc spinning like a Frisbee past the pier, beyond the bay, and out into the ocean. Then she whirled and fixed her detractor with a look.

Vincent smiled and waved back, waggling his fingers, and Emily's expression softened. Little Vinnie had given her the rage boost she'd needed to save the town from the explosion. And judging by the cheers of the rescued crowd, she'd looked good doing it.

Bug Girl didn't let Emily bask in the glory for long. Taking off (she had this down now), she grasped Emily under the arms and wheeled out over the ocean, picking up speed.

"We've got to get our moms out of that thing before it blows!" she shouted.

30

The Exterminator's last-ditch detonation vehicle bobbed on the waves, several miles from the coast and Oyster Cove. Bug Girl touched down on the smooth black surface and released her grip on her partner. The eye that had been their mothers' prison was now the cockpit of this new craft. She could see Megawoman and Dragonfly clearly, still bound and gagged inside. Standing between them, The Exterminator waved and tried to crack his haggard face into a smile. *Jerk.*

But the computerized countdown continued: forty-four . . . forty-three . . . forty-two . . .

Bug Girl didn't know a thing about deactivating bombs. What she did know was that she had to free their mothers before they were blown to bits.

"Emily, punch the roof off. We're going to need it to get out of here," Bug Girl said. A plan was forming. . . .

In a whir, Emily slammed through the roof as if she were opening a can of soup, drilling her fists in a wide circle all the way around. She ripped the perforated top free and flung it into the water beside the ailing craft, where it bobbed like a raft. Thirty-two . . . thirty-one . . . thirty . . .

Meanwhile, Bug Girl ruptured the glass of the cockpit with her handy-dandy tymbals. As soon as the glass split, water began streaming into the vehicle, but that did not slow Bug Girl. She rushed inside and grabbed her still-bound mother and then Emily's, flinging them out of the sinking ship. Then, begrudgingly, she rescued The Exterminator. "You're lucky I'm nice," she said to the grouchy geezer as he glared at her, waving his arms wildly and yelling insults.

Twenty-three . . . twenty-two . . .

Emily, who had jumped onto the getaway flotsam, caught each of the individuals as they were ejected through the portal and hauled them aboard the makeshift dinghy. The bomb craft began to sink, and Bug Girl fluttered out to take her place at the bow of the roof raft.

"Emily! Get in the water. I need you to be the rudder," she called.

Seventeen . . . sixteen . . .

Bug Girl flapped. She beat her wings as fast as she could, propelling the raft over the water.

Ten . . . nine . . .

"Kick!" Bug Girl yelled to Emily. "Get it moving, already! COME ON!"

Emily didn't care for Bug Girl's tone. Agitated, she fluttered her feet at maximum power—which sped things up considerably. In no time at all (4.2 seconds, to be exact) they were a safe distance from the ship's crash-down site.

The Exterminator screeched as the choppy water splashed in his face. "You even ruined my Contingency Phase! I'll see that you pay for this if it's the last thing I do!"

"Yeesh. Do you *ever* stop? No one cares!" Bug Girl shouted, still concentrating on getting them away from the explosive.

"Yeah, put a cork in it!" Emily added, not wanting to miss out on the fun of tormenting their captive.

They were about a mile away when the sinking ship's timer went off. The surface of the ocean churned slightly, some lazy bubbles gurgled forth, accompanied by a puff or two of smoke, and then the waters went back to their regularly scheduled ebb and flow.

"Some bomb," Emily guffawed.

The Exterminator's shoulders slumped. "I can't be perfect at everything," he managed to say before covering his face with his hands.

Emily and Bug Girl knelt down beside their mothers, Megawoman and Dragonfly, who were still bound by The Exterminator's magical spider thread. The moms' eyes were no longer filled with terror, but with absolute and beaming pride.

"Okay, Bug Girl," Emily said, pointing to the binds. "Cough up some of those potent loogies."

"Stop calling them that!" Bug Girl snorted. She and Emily helped the mothers stand up, and then, with concentration, she spat precision bombardier beetle spittle. As Bug Girl's acid weakened the binds, Emily pulled them apart, snapping the compromised threads. Finally, Oyster Cove's beloved superheroes, and Emily and Amanda's beloved mothers, wrapped their arms around their daughters and saviors! They were free. They were safe.

The group was still a good distance from the shore when a police boat caught up to them. Frida—dressed in a military uniform with a swish red beret and matching lipstick—Poppy, and Vincent were all aboard, along with several police officers who snatched the deflated Exterminator up and handcuffed him, dragging him into a cell somewhere deep within the ship's hull.

"Take me away. I'm too embarrassed," The Exterminator whined, his lips pulling back as he began to cry.

"Ugh, those teeth," Emily groaned, hiding her face in her mother's cape.

"Candy corn," Bug Girl said, nodding. "They look like candy corn. The brown kind."

Emily and Bug Girl giggled together for the first time in over a year.

Amanda hugged her mom tighter than she ever had in her entire life. She looked over and saw Emily doing the same. There were even tears streaming down Emily's face.

"Oh, honey, we are so proud of you," Amanda's mother said, pulling back enough to get a good look at her. "Thank you for saving us. I knew you could do it."

The four heroes stood on the boat's deck and watched as Oyster Cove came closer into view. Next to them stood the three freshest sidekicks anyone could hope for: Frida, Poppy, and Vincent, silent and beaming.

The police boat pulled up to the dock. Officers dragged The Exterminator from the bowels of the ship and prepared to load him into an armored car. He would be spending the rest of his years in a maximum-security prison where no insects were allowed. "Foul children!" he wheezed as he was pushed toward the vehicle. "Poltroons!"

Amanda stepped closer. "You know, I'm sorry about your dog and all," she admitted. "But you just can't treat living things like . . . that. You have to be nice," she explained, certain her words were falling on deaf ears.

The Exterminator was uncharacteristically silent. He was gazing at her with an odd look on his face. Like admiration. And when he spoke, Amanda was surprised.

"Bug Girl," he rasped, "may I touch your wings?"

Amanda thought of wind and clouds and kites soaring sky-high. Her wings fluttered open, and The Exterminator reached out a thin hand. His touch was gentle, and

brief. And Amanda thought she saw him smile as they closed and locked the car door.

As Bug Girl and Emily stepped off the dock, all of Oyster Cove burst into applause.

The mayor greeted the two new heroes. He brought them through the crowd to the Oyster Cove Day bandstand, where they received the ovation they deserved. Bug Girl and Emily took their bows before waving their mothers onstage with them. Citizens went even wilder, seeing their beloved Megawoman and Dragonfly freed from danger. All was well.

"Thanks to you, young heroes, our wonderful town has been saved! And Dragonfly and Megawoman have been returned. Let us celebrate these brave girls! I declare this the best Oyster Cove Day ever!"

As the townspeople cheered, clapped, and called, the four amazing superheroes stood together, proud and safe.

"You two newfangled youngsters sure showed The Exterminator a thing or two," Poppy chuckled as the heroes exited the stage. "How about a spaghetti dinner?"

"Great idea," Emily shouted. "I'm starving!"

Frida and Mrs. Battfield sandwiched the sparkly hero in a hug. "You're wrinkling my unitard," she hissed jokingly.

Vincent was too choked up to speak, but the look he gave Amanda said it all: *Dang, girl.* In contrast, Amanda's mom could not stop talking.

"Oh, Sweet Potato! Just look at you!" she gushed at Amanda. "Antennae? Wings? Oh, I could just burst! I knew it was a good idea to feed you extra protein and bee pollen. You and Emily are heroes, just as we knew you would be!" Amanda's mother squeezed both girls' shoulders. "And you are friends again, too!"

Bug Girl looked at her partner with a grin so big, it threatened to split her face—her happiness was clear.

Emily's expression was unreadable. Her smile was reserved. "About that," Emily said under her breath. "We're cool and all. But don't talk to me at school, okay?"

Bug Girl stared—her smile frozen. *Seriously?*

EPILOGUE

Amanda Price's seventh-grade year started out as expected. Terribly.

School had only been in session for a week, and Mr. Schenkenclabber had already assigned oral reports in science class. Having experienced rather strong reactions to past reports, she had chosen what she viewed as a relatively mundane topic—*Trash Bugs: Vampires of the Insect Kingdom.*

After delivering her report about the hoboesque insects that hobble around with their victims' exoskeletons piled on their backs, Amanda took her seat. Some of the students stared at her nervously, as if her topic were weird.

Then it was Vincent's turn. Amanda's best friend had chosen a more controversial topic, based on his new obsession with the exploration of the great unknown.

"Mokele-Mbembe: the Last Living Dinosaur," Vincent read aloud from the podium. "That's pronounced *Moe-kay-lay Em-bem-bay*," he repeated. Amanda gave him an encouraging look.

Vincent continued. "The last living dinosaur, a brontosaurus, to be exact, is rumored to be hiding out in the African Congo. Lake Tele, its reported home, is a massive circular body of water surrounded by near-impenetrable forest. A Japanese expedition to the lake garnered some blurry film footage, but all other explorers have either failed to reach the lake or come up with inconclusive results."

Amanda sat rapt as Vincent showed slides of what the beast was rumored to look like. She relished the idea of sharing the world with as-yet-undiscovered creatures. But apparently not everyone was as smitten with the idea.

"Who cares about some tacky dinosaur?" someone

blurted from the back. "That's about as scientific as a report on aliens. *They don't exist.* F-plus, if you ask me."

Amanda turned, a sour look on her face. You didn't interrupt Vincent Verbiglia when he was speaking as far as Amanda was concerned.

But when she saw the flap jaw that had so rudely offered unwanted commentary, she froze. The buttinsky was none other than Geraldine Atrixious, or Geri, as she had asked to be called.

Geri was a new student at Oyster Cove Middle School. She had taken the school by storm and risen through the social ranks with lightning speed. The new reigning queen was holding court at the back table, surrounded by the popular girls—every single one of whom would do Geri's bidding if she so much as crooked a little finger. Everyone, including Emily.

Although Emily and Amanda had trained together all summer, back at

school it was business as usual. That is, Emily ignored Amanda or treated her like she was gum on her shoe. Sure, it made sense when Emily explained that a shift in their behavior would call attention to them and raise suspicions, but it didn't make it hurt any less. They were partners and friends, yet Amanda had to continue to pretend otherwise. Not cool.

Amanda said nothing to Geri (nor did anyone else, including the teacher!) and gave her undivided attention to the remainder of Vincent's report. When the bell rang, she thought she might whisper *something* to Emily. But before she was close enough to speak undetected, her sensilla rang an internal alarm. Something was off. She scanned the in-crowd and noticed that Mikki Folders was missing. Come to mention it, Sadie Bimmins was absent, too, and hadn't been to school in several days. No one else seemed to think this was unusual, but Amanda certainly did. Her bug powers were telling her that things were not right. And her instincts were pointing toward one thing: Geri.

Bug Girl sensed danger. And she was ready. *Was Emily?*

About the Authors

Sarah Hines Stephens has been a children's book reader, editor, seller, buyer, doctor, author, copyeditor, ghostwriter, and speaker for many years—and she is still most of those things. She makes her home in Oakland, California, where she lives with her husband, two kids, and two dogs.

Benjamin Harper has been involved in children's books as both an editor and author, ever since he graduated from Warren Wilson College. Currently, he lives in Los Angeles, California, where he works on superhero stories and lives with his cat, Edith Bouvier Beale, III.

ACKNOWLEDGMENTS

A long time ago in an attic on a ranch far, far away, the idea for *Bug Girl* was hatched. The two of us met working as children's book editors at Lucasfilm in 1999. We became fast friends and knew it would be fun to write together. We talked about the idea for *Bug Girl* off and on for years and finally penned the first draft in 2006. Since then, *Bug Girl* has gone through many changes and never would have emerged as a book without the guidance and help of many people. We'd like to extend a special thank-you to Erin Stein for letting *Bug Girl* fly, as well as Ellen Duda, Elissa Englund, Melinda Ackell, Nicole Otto, and everyone else at Imprint Books and Macmillan who assisted with the metamorphosis.

We would like to thank Lucy Autrey Wilson for bringing us together all those years ago, Sue Rostoni for being fabulous, and all those who read early versions of *Bug Girl* and offered advice. We are grateful.

B.H. & S.H.S.

I'd like to thank my parents, Frances and Jeffrey Harper, for encouraging me to be a weirdo and also for helping me to hatch many a praying mantis egg case and butterfly cocoon over the years (and my father for allowing me to swipe the name "Mega-woman," a character he created in the 1970s!); Sarah Hines Stephens for being a wonderful writing partner and amazing friend; Mary-Kate Gaudet for everything; Steve Korté, Allison Harper, Josh Anderson, and Margaret Evans for reading early and very different versions of this book; Nizzles; and everyone out there who, when faced with a Madagascar hissing cockroach or a walking stick, says "awesome!" instead of "GROSS."

B.H.

I want to thank Ben, of course: I'm so glad you charmed me with your sunny scowl and perfect mix tapes. I only wish we'd met in middle school! I'd also like to thank Jane Mason—another great friendship forged in that attic far, far away. Jane, thanks for being my ear, reader, and shoulder. Ian, Sarah J., Emmett, and especially Violet and Ada, you were supreme listeners 'round the campfire, on the couch, and in the car. Thanks for your feedback—you're Bug Girl's (and The Exterminator's) first fans! Mom and Gary, you are my first fans. Thank you for your love, support, encouragement, and example. (And Popa, I totally forgive you for killing any spiders and insects breaching the house when I was a kid.) And finally, Nathan, my very own pencil-neck-geek-turned-hero-husband, thanks for building me up, breaking it down, and for always, and for everything.

S.H.S.